THE
PHANTOM'S
CURSE

SHELLEY WILSON

THE
PHANTOM'S
CURSE

A NOVEL

bhc
press™

Livonia, Michigan

Edited by Susan Cunningham
Proofread by Lana King and Jamie Rich

THE PHANTOM'S CURSE

Published by BHC Press

Library of Congress Control Number:
2020931374

ISBN: 978-1-64397-071-4 (Hardcover)
ISBN: 978-1-64397-091-2 (Softcover)
ISBN: 978-1-64397-092-9 (Ebook)

For information, write:
BHC Press
885 Penniman #5505
Plymouth, MI 48170

Visit the publisher:
www.bhcpress.com

ALSO BY
SHELLEY WILSON

Hood Academy

The Guardians Series

Guardians of the Dead
Book 1 of The Guardians

Guardians of the Sky
Book 2 of The Guardians

Guardians of the Lost Lands
Book 3 of The Guardians

For Nikki.

Thank you for the coffee and counsel.

When battling a curse it's always good
to have a friend to call upon.

THE
PHANTOM'S
CURSE

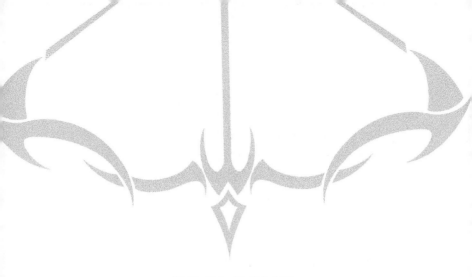

PROLOGUE

Nobody could command the phantom once it occupied a host body. The old magic and the corrupt mages who wielded its supremacy called forth a power so evil, believing they could contain it and manipulate the host to do their bidding, but they were wrong.

The tendrils of darkness that seeped into the once innocent mind of their lord's daughter, Lady Lindley, infected her thoughts, twisted her ideals, and ripped her soul apart.

Instead of controlling the shadow magic as the mages believed they could, it demolished everything in its path.

Lady Lindley became a puppet of malevolence, a scourge upon the realm. She terrorised the people, murdered the mages and devoured them all.

At her hand, the black magic swept through the old world like a tsunami. It cleansed the land of man, woman, and child, and no one was safe. No one could survive the ferocity of the phantom's curse as it delivered destruction through the hands of a young girl.

The earth bled, the clouds wept, and everyone died.

Almost everyone.

A young soldier named Davis Reign and his friend Cassias, a fledgeling sorcerer, sought to defeat the phantom and drive the darkness back into the bowels of hell freeing their lady from its grasp. The people rose with them, bolstered by the hope that Davis Reign would succeed where the corrupt mages had failed.

The lands ran with rivers of blood as the young friends battled the oldest evil. Bloodied, exhausted, and beaten they retreated into the lower chambers of the castle. Time was against them, and Lady Lindley's ferocity grew with every swing of a sword, but as they fled through the crypt they discovered the trapped soul of their true lady, her pure white light imprisoned in a cage of fire. Using the last of their physical and emotional strength they ripped her soul free, watching it rise through the floors, seeking to be reunited with its physical body.

The lady stood atop a pile of corpses. Blood dripped from her sword and she screamed in fury as wave upon wave of soldiers advanced on the city. A great roar came from beneath the ground as the young soldier and his sorcerer friend emerged from the rubble and devastation that surrounded them, daggers drawn. They didn't hesitate despite the furious roar of the phantom as it battled against their lady's pure soul. The young girl was losing the internal battle between good and evil as the phantom fought to stay in its host, and it would have won if Davis Reign hadn't buried his blade into the lady's heart.

She died in his arms surrounded by the death and bloodshed she had administered, but with a look of peace and relief etched on her once beautiful features. With her death, the sun returned to the sky, and a young soldier was thrust to the forefront and handed the role of the people's saviour.

From the darkness, a new power arose. Davis Reign claimed the title of Lord of Obanac and with Cassias's help built wards to keep the darkness buried and ensure the safety of the inhabitants who had survived this plague of black magic.

Once the ashes settled and the old ways were forgotten, Davis and Cassias rebuilt the great city through the sweat and tears of the common man. They embraced the lower towns, the plains, and the mountain regions, which were the worst hit by the savagery of the phantom's curse, extending the magical wards and uniting the people from all the realms.

For a time there was peace and tranquillity throughout the land, and when Davis married a young girl from the Link, one of the lower towns under the protection of the city, it looked like that unity would continue to thrive. No longer would the realm be divided. Davis loved and laughed, and he honoured the people by keeping them safe. The citizens across the realm trusted in him and his rule, but there was a force working against him. A force that had once shared his confidence and friendship. His old friend grew jealous of the love Davis had for Lucy Reign and the time he spent with her. He grew more and more disconnected as the years went by, choosing to spend his time deep in the bowels of the castle.

If Davis had taken the time to listen, he would have heard the whispers from the wilds, the plains, the murmurings from the mountains, and the tiny flutter of discontent that was building in the lower towns.

Something was stirring beneath the earth once again. The pure mages could sense it, and those who had survived the phantom's curse feared a repeat of the dark past.

As Lucy and Davis welcomed a son into the world, they believed that nothing could destroy the happiness and contentment they felt. The people of Obanac were swept up in the Lord's euphoria, but the pure mages knew. They understood.

When Lucy Reign breathed her last just three years later, it broke the lord's heart, and the careful threads of peace began to unravel. The whispers became stronger as the voices across the lands spoke as one. They shouted a warning of what was to come, but their lord was too wracked with grief to care.

The lands suffered at the hands of a shattered lord. Corrupt advisors stepped into power and divided them once again. At their suggestion, they pulled back the wards that protected the plains and the lower towns leaving them exposed to any threat of dark magic. They used the lord's grief for their own financial gain by protecting the city and keeping its riches safe. Davis forgot who he had been fighting for and in their thirst to control the lord, his advisors divided the citizens, turning neighbour against neighbour, brother against brother, and tearing children from the arms of their parents.

The city of Obanac became a sanctuary for the wealthy and influential. Towns like the Link, together with the villages on the plains, descended into poverty.

By the time Davis Reign died the realm was unrecognisable. When his son stepped up as heir the city advisors wore smug smiles believing they could contain the young lord and mould him to suit their own needs. The days of the old mages and their quest for supremacy were returning. The residents of Obanac were oblivious to what was unfolding, but the people beyond the city walls understood and protected the lower towns and the plains with wards of their own. They feared that nobody was strong enough to stop what was coming, but they were wrong.

The pure mages knew there was one person who could bring them all out of the shadows and back into the light. Only she could reunite the realms.

So, they waited.

ONE

'It's not fair!' Newt squirmed in my grasp as I tried to drag the comb through his dirty hair. 'No one else has to suffer this kind of torture.'

I cracked a smile as the comb snagged on a matted clump and he yelped.

'We've got to look decent to go into the city, Newt, you know that. The nice folk won't let in a scruffy urchin.'

Newt's shoulders sagged as he admitted defeat. 'Why do we have to go inside the city? Why can't the city folks come and visit us here instead?'

I set down the comb on an upturned crate and turned him to face me. His big hazel eyes studied my expression, as if searching for the wisdom he believed was there.

For years I'd tried my hardest to be the person he needed. To be a wise big sister as well as mother, father, and mentor. Davis Reign had sent our parents away without any warning, and I had stepped up to the task without a murmur. My brother was the only thing I had left in the world, and I took my role as his protector seriously.

'They don't come out to the Link, Newt, you remember what I told you? They're still scared of leaving the protective wards the lord put up around Obanac. The phantom's magic tore this world apart, and some folk remember those times.'

Looking past my brother's shoulder, I stared out at the dirt road that cut through the bedraggled self-built village. The earlier rain had settled into black puddles along the track, and the mud resembled thick tar. I wondered if the streets of Obanac looked like these, or if they gleamed as bright as the city workers told me.

A cart trundled past flinging the sticky earth into the air as its wheels spun slowly. The jolt of the wagon brought me back to the present.

Newt was squirming on the small bed, tugging at the collar of his borrowed shirt. I pulled him close and wrapped my arm around his shoulder.

'It's only for a couple of hours. We'll be back in the Link before you know it. Besides, it's a great honour to get an invitation to the blessing. Old Mrs Elrod used to work in the city, and she's always telling me how much she misses visiting.'

'Well you can tell Mrs E that she can go instead of me if she wants,' he mumbled.

I couldn't help but laugh at his miserable expression.

'Come on, sulky, let's get it over with.'

The townsfolk of the Link had gathered to watch us leave, and I felt oddly conspicuous as we all shuffled down the main street. Men and women who had been friends with our parents nodded their approval, and children I had helped look after splashed through the puddles as they ran alongside us on the track. It was a momentous occasion when a resident of the lower towns turned sixteen and could visit the sparkling glory of Obanac, but it didn't make the entire situation any less uncomfortable. Being the centre of attention was something I despised, and my gut reaction was to turn and run even though the gathered crowds were friends not foes.

I tugged at the sleeves of my dress and moved my hands to smooth down the bodice that clung to every curve and line of my body. Perhaps that's why I felt so awkward. I was used to dressing in trousers and a baggy shirt with my bow and arrows and hunting daggers strapped to my back. Wearing an eye-catching fitted dress with matching green pumps and leaving my long, fiery red hair to fall around my shoulders wasn't a normal look for me.

'You look lovely, my dear.' A petite grey-haired woman in a long purple cloak broke through the crowds and rushed to my side, grasping my hands in her gnarled ones and squeezing tightly. 'A vision of beauty and grace. Your parents would be so proud.'

Her eyes glossed over and I had to fight the urge to shed my own tears. My parents had taught me so much about surviving in the Link, but they never taught me how to survive without them by my side.

'Thank you, Mrs E.'

'Are you nervous?'

I shook my head. 'Not really. Father told me so much about the castle from when he worked there that I can picture it stone by stone.'

My childhood bedtime stories hadn't been tales of fairy-tale princesses; instead, they had involved detailed schematics of the city, its streets and houses, and its main courtyard. Our father helped to rebuild the great castle and the surrounding buildings that sat at the very heart of the warded metropolis. He was proud of his work, and I was honoured that he wanted to share the details with me. Even as a young child I understood how hard Father worked to bring us the food, cloth, and essentials we needed as a family.

'Well, your pa was one of the finest architects Obanac has ever seen, so I've no doubt you'll recognise his work when you're there.'

I smiled down at the old woman who had been in my life for as long as I could remember. Her story was still told around the campfires at night. How she had survived the phantom's magic wave which killed her entire family, and how after years of wandering the plains she was welcomed into the city by the enigmatic Lucy Reign. Mrs Elrod's skills as a seamstress were the stuff of legends and the inhabitants of Obanac had flocked to her for their lavish garments.

'I wish you could come with us,' I whispered, squeezing the old woman's hands in return.

'I know,' Mrs Elrod replied, a sad smile on her wrinkly face. 'But the city dream ended for me when Lucy died. Our young lord would hang me if I ever took a step over the threshold.'

My old friend seemed excited yet apprehensive about the blessing and my trip into the city, and I could only assume it was because she had been banished on pain of death by the lord's father many years ago.

I'd only ever known Mrs Elrod as a friend of my parents. The time she spent in Obanac was over when I was born. We had all tried over the years to get her to talk about it, but the old lady remained silent, only ever retelling the stories that everyone already knew. The tales of dark magic, evil curses, and of young Lady Lindley who destroyed the world. Those were the yarns that kept the children engaged and the old folk fearful.

On occasion, when she let her guard down, or if I'd managed to get hold of some wine from a merchant, Mrs Elrod would talk about Lucy Reign and how beautiful and kind she was. I'd listen to her stories as if she was talking about a princess from a faraway land, filled with wonder about the strawberry blonde beauty from the Link who married the brave Lord of Obanac. She had been a healer just like me and then one day her life changed forever when she fell in love with a lord.

'*Not everyone has goodness in them,*' my mother used to tell me. '*And if they do it can be stripped away. Look at what happened to Davis Reign. After Lucy's death, the Lord of Obanac changed and the realm changed with him.*'

These were the stories told around the campfires now. I longed to hear the tales of promise, love, and peace, but it seemed nobody wanted to hear about a fantasy. They wanted real-life tragedy.

I'd made it my mission to get Mrs Elrod to tell me the truth about Lucy Reign's death, but so far she'd remained tight-lipped. I wasn't sure why I cared so much. I guess I'd always held out some faint hope that there was more to life than my own drab existence in the lower towns, but the older I got the further away that dream felt.

Hearing my mother talk about the years before Newt and I were born was always a highlight for me, and it brought that magical time to life.

'*Davis Reign was a reasonable man with a warm and generous nature,*' she would tell us. '*He devoted his time to gathering valuable assets from the old world, and recycling them for the benefit of the people.*' I'd pull the blankets up to my chin and listen to her account of a young soldier who saved our realm. A dark-haired boy who took on the momentous role of protector. When I lay awake at night, I would fantasise about meeting a fearless boy who would love me as much as Davis had loved his Lucy.

'Now, I don't want you to be nervous.' Mrs Elrod pulled me from my musings. 'The lord is only a couple of years older than you, so I'll bet he's just as anxious about the blessing as the lads and lasses attending.'

As Mrs Elrod guided me along the main street with Newt dragging his heels behind me, I wondered once again about our young lord, Crawford Reign.

When Crawford stepped out of the crypt promising to continue in his father's footsteps, the city folk had rejoiced, but the whispers that filtered through to the lower towns, and out across the plains, spoke of a lord who was too young to rule and only had his own interests at heart.

That was four years ago, and he was still the ruling Lord of Obanac.

He must be doing something right.

Even though the blessing was everything I hated as an introvert, I had butterflies in the pit of my stomach at the thought of meeting Crawford Reign in person. I'd watched him whenever he rode out of the castle with his holy man, or when he took his elite guard on a training exercise, and I'd seen him walking the high walls surrounding the city. But I'd never been so close that I could see the colour of his eyes.

'Davis Reign's eyes turned to stone when Lucy died,' Mother told me one night. 'Something broke inside him, and he hardened his heart to the people who relied on him so much.'

'How can anyone love someone so much that it causes that much pain when they're gone?' I'd asked her.

My mother had laughed and told me that one day I'd understand.

When Davis Reign's elite guard tore our parents from our arms that same week, I finally understood the lesson. They were loaded aboard two carts destined for opposite ends of the realm, and my heart had broken. Davis had been swayed by his advisors to manipulate the people, disrupt the status quo, and keep the residents of the lower towns on their knees, but something inside me changed that day, and instead of feeling weak I learned how to be strong. Newt needed a sister who could look after him, and that was all that mattered.

I looked behind me to check my brother was still there. His sullen face made me chuckle as we followed the growing crowds heading for the castle gates.

We trudged along the main street toward the gleaming city walls which towered above us. Mage Hall greeted me at the outer limits by the huge iron gates. It was the only part of the city anyone from the lower towns was allowed to visit. Without an official invitation from the lord, a merchant's licence, or a contract of employment the iron gates remained closed to the outside world.

'It's a special day for you, Marianne, and your friends and family here in the Link are so proud of you.'

I smiled up at the mage and marvelled once again at how similar our features were. When I was born with a mass of red curls and eyes as green as the meadow, the mage had proclaimed that I was one of them. A healer and magic maker. If there was any magic simmering beneath my skin I'd never felt it, but my confidence as a healer was growing. Only yesterday I'd helped a group of merchants who had been attacked on the plains as they moved from town to town.

'Enjoy your day inside the city walls but remember where your heart resides.'

I would have thought that an odd thing for the mage to say had Mrs Elrod not forewarned me about the residents of Obanac and their desire to recruit new blood from the lower towns to work in their homes and look after their affairs.

'We'll *both* be home in a few hours, Mage Hall, I promise.'

He smiled and moved aside so I could see the gate.

Ahead of the fancy ironwork lay a long track furrowed by cartwheels. On either side of the road deep craters packed with jagged rocks and choking vines stretched as far as the eye could see, wrapping themselves around the city like a waterless moat. Beyond the craters were the inner wall and the gatehouse where the city officials and the Lord of Obanac would meet us. A bridge would then take us over the river of tar that hugged the main walls. The city's defence against mankind was almost as absolute as the wards against black magic that shimmered along the length of the walls.

Newt slid his hand into mine.

'Ready?' I asked, squeezing his fingers.

'Ready!' he said.

We took a tentative step forward as a loud cry filled the air. I spun on my heel to see three boys my age scrambling through the crowds. The audible tut from Mrs Elrod raised a grin on the lead boy's handsome face as he winked at her before pushing forward to where I stood with Newt.

'Hey kiddo, looking good.' He ruffled Newt's hair, which made my brother laugh, but I slapped his hand away and began smoothing down the strands that had taken on a life of their own.

'Leave him alone,' I snapped, glaring up into the newcomer's big blue eyes. 'I've warned you already. If you don't leave my brother alone I'll...'

'You'll what?' He took another step closer until I could feel his breath on my skin. Heat rushed up my neck and speckled my cheeks, but I refused to step away.

'My brother is not here for your amusement, Robbie. He's just a boy, and I don't want him following you on your foolish raids.'

'Foolish? Who was it that got you those pretty green shoes you're wearing? Oh yes, that would be your brother and me on one of our silly raids.'

'Yes, and it got him whipped by the market trader who recognised him!'

'An unfortunate development,' Robbie said as he spun in a wide circle clearly enjoying being the centre of attention for the gathered crowd. 'But while Newt was taking his beating we were able to swipe a roll of cloth that Mrs E didn't grumble about.'

At the mention of her name, Mrs Elrod shuffled forward and shooed Robbie an arm's length away from me.

'You need to leave this young lad alone for a while. He needs to support Marianne because mage only knows what awaits her after the blessing.'

He glanced between me and the fortress that stretched out before us.

'You're really going in there?' He jerked his thumb in the direction of the city walls before leaning in closer. 'Are you crazy?'

'I've just turned sixteen, Robbie, I've been summoned. Besides, it's only for a few hours, and then I'll be back in the Link where I belong.'

'I never got my invitation when I turned sixteen,' he said with a wink.

I shook my head but couldn't help the smile that tugged at the corner of my mouth. 'Maybe it's because you stole the lord's pig!'

'He didn't know for certain that it was me,' he said with a chuckle.

I turned away and gestured for Newt to follow, but Robbie was fast and manoeuvred himself into our path once again.

'There's been another attack on the plains,' he whispered, leaning closer so my brother couldn't hear.

A heavy weight pressed down on my chest as I listened to Robbie's retelling of the morning assault by the vile murderers known only as the Black Riders. The raids on the villages out on the plains were becoming more frequent, and as a healer, it fell upon my shoulders to see to any injuries.

'Why are you telling me this now?'

Robbie took a step back as if I'd struck him.

'It's your responsibility to help our people,' he said. 'You know what's going on in the realm and we need your help. This is no time for fluffy dresses and flirting with the lord's guards.'

I lifted my head and looked directly into Robbie's eyes. They shone like bright blue agate in the early morning sun. The furrows across his brow and the downward tilt to his jaw showed me how offended he was that I was choosing the blessing over our people.

'I *have* to go to the blessing, Robbie, it's dangerous for everyone in the Link if I refuse the lord's invitation.'

'It's more dangerous to leave the plains unprotected. The Black Riders could turn their attention on the Link or even on your precious city folk at any moment.'

I turned away from him, not wanting to listen to his petty whining any longer, but he grabbed my arm, pulling me close.

'I would never want you to be in any danger,' he said quietly, 'but our people are dying, and we need to do something.'

'I'll only be gone a few hours, Robbie, and then I'll ride to the plains and help, okay?'

I gave him a tight smile and turned toward the iron gates, their size feeling even more overwhelming all of a sudden.

'Don't bother,' he grumbled before stomping off in the direction of his friends.

I don't know why Robbie's reaction upset me so much. He was notorious in the lower towns for being a trickster and a thief, but the residents tolerated him because his father had been a well-respected man. Unfortunately, like most of the kids in the lower towns and out on the plains, having good parents didn't get you anywhere. Robbie, together with his sidekicks Fergus and Xander, tore up the rulebook and decided to live outside of the law, and that made them dangerous regardless of any good intentions they had.

If any of them were to step inside the city walls, they would never come out again. The lord would throw them all in a cell and leave them to rot. It troubled me that I felt compelled to help Robbie with this quest of his to save the people, but it troubled me more that Newt only saw the excitement and adventure that Robbie promised.

I wanted to believe that he would protect my brother, but in reality he was the type who only looked after himself.

Mrs Elrod stood before us breaking into my thoughts.

'Time to go,' she said, waving a wrinkled hand in the direction of the gatehouse and the city walls. 'I'll be waiting for you when you get home,' she told us holding me in a warm embrace.

I blinked away the tears that pooled in the corners of my eyes. I didn't know why I was so emotional or why I had the strangest feeling we were saying goodbye for the last time.

'I'll see you soon,' I replied, glancing in the direction Robbie had gone.

He stood at the back of the crowd with his arms folded across his chest and the hilt of his sword just visible over his shoulder. His scowl made my chest tight, and I berated myself for allowing him to make me feel that way.

Fergus and Xander had already moved off down the main street toward the town's market square and were calling to their friend, but he kept his gaze fixed on me, his eyes smouldering.

I grabbed Newt's hand and we strode down the track, headed for the city. I resisted the temptation to look back as a deep feeling of dread flooded my system. I didn't know where it came from, but as we approached the gatehouse, I had an overwhelming sensation of never seeing the Link, Mrs Elrod, or Robbie again.

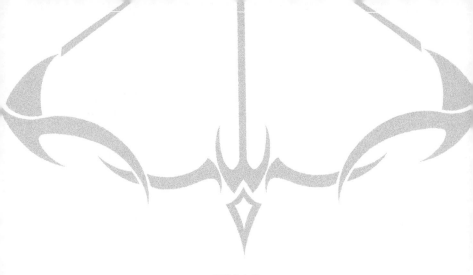

TWO

'**Y**ou! What's your name?'

My shoulders folded in on themselves as I squirmed beneath the lord's steely glare. I didn't appreciate being the centre of attention and found myself holding my breath as Crawford Reign approached.

My foolish young girl's wish had been granted; the young Lord of Obanac was standing in front of me, and all I wanted to do was run the other way.

In Mother's stories she'd talked about the many people who believed that being only a boy was Crawford's weakness, but as I bristled under his cold gaze, I couldn't sense any limitations, only power and confidence.

'Marianne,' I whispered.

With my voice so quiet the lord leaned in closer causing a shudder to skitter along my spine. I didn't know why my skin was crawling or why I had an overpowering urge to flee, but I couldn't deny my gut reactions. The sensations were unexpected, and I hoped my face didn't reflect the revulsion that washed over me.

'M a r i a n n e.' He rolled every letter over his tongue as he spoke my name making it sound soiled to my ears. I vowed there and then to never use my full name again.

'I haven't seen you in the city before, Marianne, who do you live with?'

'I don't live in the city, my lord, I'm from the Link.'

A twitch of a smile rearranged his features for the briefest moment. If I hadn't been looking directly at him I would have missed it.

He recovered himself and adjusted the clasp on his cloak. His eyes were as black as the night sky, and the dark shadow of stubble dusting his chin detracted from his pale complexion. He was strikingly handsome but in a chiselled-from-granite way, not in the warm and homely way that Robbie was handsome.

I mentally kicked myself for thinking about Robbie. That boy drove me crazy with his wild and reckless manner.

'How lovely,' Crawford said, taking me by the elbow and leading me to a quieter spot. 'So, this is your first visit inside the walls.'

I remained quiet. It was a statement rather than a question.

'Who is your escort today?' He scanned the crowd clearly searching for a parent, guardian, or partner who would claim me.

'I'm with my brother, my lord.' I motioned for Newt to make himself known and as he stumbled forward into full view, his hair flopped into his eyes. With an exasperated sigh he blew his fringe out of the way and grinned up at the lord.

Crawford Reign chuckled.

'He's nervous,' I said trying to draw away the lord's attention before Newt embarrassed me any more, 'but as my only remaining family it fell on him to be my companion for the blessing.'

Crawford nodded his understanding.

'We've all lost so much,' he said, dragging his gaze along the outline of my body.

I shuddered at his scrutiny but gave a polite nod. 'Yes, my lord.'

'As you're now sixteen it means you can gain employment in the city. I trust you have someone who will look after your brother's interests.' He waved his hand in Newt's direction.

'I intend to stay in the Link, my lord, and continue my work as a healer so I'm still able to look after my brother.'

There was no way I would want to live in the city, but I didn't dare tell the Lord of Obanac that minor detail. Putting my childhood fantasies aside, I knew I had no intention of leaving Newt behind.

'Admirable quality,' he said. 'Let's hope it's the right decision.'

Crawford shifted his attention to a nearby guard with a long scar along his cheek. They exchanged words, and the guard studied Newt and me before giving a curt nod and moving off without another word.

'I hope you enjoy your day in Obanac, Marianne.' Crawford lifted my hand and kissed it then disappeared into the crowds.

Newt let out a whooshing breath once Crawford Reign was out of range and my shoulders dropped from their tense position up by my ears.

'Glad that's over,' Newt said, pulling on my hand. 'Can we go home now?'

'Not yet, we've got to have a celebratory feast in the great hall. All the food you can eat.'

I was still a little shaky after meeting the lord, but I prayed it wasn't obvious in my voice. We'd only just begun the blessing festivities, and I hoped the promise of food would change the miserable set of his little jaw, but Newt didn't look impressed.

'I don't want to eat city food and sit with city folk. They smell.'

I giggled. 'They don't smell, Newt.'

'They do!' He pulled me closer and leaned in as if he was sharing a precious secret. 'They stink of flowers.'

'That's soap, Newt. The city folk are just cleaner than you.'

'Well, it's not normal,' he said, crossing his arms over his borrowed jacket and surveying the crowd. 'What's so wrong with a bit of muck?'

I was about to reprimand him when Crawford Reign's booming voice carried across the open space.

'Welcome to Obanac.' There was rapturous applause from the city dwellers, who were accustomed to pomp and ceremony when the lord spoke. 'Let's begin the celebrations.'

The claps and cheers carried us along as we followed Crawford Reign and the soldiers out of the gatehouse and across the long moat bridge suspended above the tar pit. The dark stone of the castle entrance towered above us as we entered the city.

Newt's fingers tightened on mine as we passed under the sharp teeth of the portcullis glinting high above our heads.

'Don't worry, Newt, you're safe with me. Stay by my side, and we'll get through this day together, okay?'

He nodded in confirmation as his eyes widened at the sights and sounds around us.

Through the main gate crowds had gathered to welcome the assembly for the blessing. Brightly coloured flags strung across the small entrance fluttered high above as the nervous congregation shuffled through to stand within the city walls. The cobblestones shone like polished brass, and bright red flowers filled two huge stone urns just inside the gate.

I'd never seen anything so beautiful in my life. To the left, a grassy embankment rose up to meet the castle which towered above us on the crest of the hill. On our right, a small orchard with abundant apple trees stretched all the way up to a long, single-story building with the lord's crest hanging above the entrance. I remembered from Father's stories that this was the courthouse, a place for the lord to inflict his justice upon any wrongdoer.

Our party continued to follow the cobblestone path as it wound between the grass ridge and the courthouse. It deviated sharply to the left passing some larger stone buildings. At every window a shiny face peered out at the passing parade. Some cheered and waved, others melted into the shadows as the procession ambled by.

A lavish garden appeared ahead of us crammed with every variety of flower and herb imaginable. Neatly trimmed hedges bordered the entire space with an arched entrance carved out of overhanging branches. The volume of medicinal herbs that grew by the side of the path was overwhelming. It took me weeks to forage for plants and roots to help heal my patients and yet here in the city the borders were overflowing with everything they could need. I swallowed my resentfulness and followed the rest of the party. Crawford Reign and his guards entered the garden and ascended the stone steps that led up to the castle's main door. They stopped at the top, and the lord raised his arms to silence the crowds as he addressed the assembled party.

'Welcome to my home.' He cast a predatory gaze over the crowd as if deciding whether he should let us in or not. 'I ask that you enjoy the celebrations and the feast, but refrain from touching the art or collections. My father prided himself on filling this castle with treasures from the old world, and I hope that you can honour his memory by respecting my wishes.'

I was stunned by the beauty of the surroundings and quite moved by Crawford's speech. Was I wrong in my initial assessment of the Lord of Obanac? Did he sound genuinely choked up as he spoke about his father or were these false emotions used to manipulate the crowds?

'I have tried to carry on the good work Davis Reign started, and as such, I ask that you don't wander away from the party, or steal anything that belongs to the city.'

His gaze strayed briefly to where I stood with Newt near the back of the crowd, and I groaned inwardly. Any illusion I'd dreamed up about the lord's compassion fizzled out as he locked eyes with me. He thought we would steal from him. Everything we did and said during the ceremony would be done under the watchful eye of the lord and his elite guards. They would be scrutinising our every movement in case we ran off with a priceless heirloom.

'Ow, you're hurting me,' Newt hissed through gritted teeth as he tried to wriggle free of my grasp.

I hadn't realised I'd been squeezing his hand so tight and quickly relaxed my posture. Anger bubbled in the pit of my stomach as we watched Crawford Reign wave a gloved hand and enter through the large wooden doors. He didn't trust us because we were from the Link, but that division between the wealth of the city and the poverty of the lower towns was on him and his father. They were the ones responsible for the lack of unity across the realm. I looked around for the first time and studied the other members of the blessing party.

There were three girls, including myself, and seven boys in the celebration. Their clean clothes, tidy hair, and soft hands identified them as city dwellers. I was the only resident of the lower towns. Unease flooded my system as we filed up the stone steps after the others. If anything went wrong at the party, then we would be targeted.

Before we reached the top step, I pulled Newt close and whispered in his ear.

'Stay by my side at all times and only do what I say, do you understand me?'

His eyes widened at the severe look on my face. 'What's wrong?'

I tried to relax my facial expression with a smile.

'Nothing, I just don't want us getting into any trouble as it's such a special day.'

'I'll be on my best behaviour.' He spat in his palm and held it high waiting for me to do the same. It was our secret pact and had cemented many a decision.

I glanced after the group retreating inside the castle and spat into my palm, slapping it against Newt's.

'Let's get this over with then.'

I kept a tight hold of Newt's sticky hand as we walked into the lion's den.

The great hall was exactly that: great. Great in size, decoration, and splendour. A long table had been set up at the far end of the room where Crawford Reign and his entourage were seated. Two further tables branched off it and stretched down the full length of the hall.

I couldn't make out what kind of wood the tables were made of as every inch of the tops were covered in food and flowers. A large roasted pig was the centrepiece of each station, surrounded by potatoes, steaming vegetables, and freshly baked loaves of bread.

Goblets of wine were handed out to the adults in the party, who sloshed them in the air as they saluted the group.

Guards began to usher the guests to their seats, and in the rush I lost my grip on Newt's hand. I spun around in a panic searching for him, but the hall was full of people jostling in all directions to secure a good seat close to the lord. Dread settled in my chest like a rock and tears welled up behind my eyes. We hadn't even lasted five minutes without something going wrong.

'Don't worry, your brother will be looked after by the serving staff.'

The soft voice coaxed me out of my panic and pulled my attention back to the present. A young man of about my age stood close by. He had big brown gentle eyes and cropped brown hair. When he smiled tiny dimples showed in his cheeks.

'See, he's already making himself at home.' The boy nodded at a smaller table off to the rear of the room. A group of younger children were busy tucking into roast chicken seemingly oblivious to the excited chatter of the other guests.

I let out the breath I'd been holding in and visibly relaxed my shoulders. The sick feeling that had washed over me dissipated. Newt was giggling with a girl wearing blue ribbons in her hair while licking the grease off his slim fingers.

'Thank you,' I murmured, feeling suddenly vulnerable. 'He's the only family I've got, and I worry about him all the time.'

The boy smiled, and his entire face lit up.

'I've never had any brothers or sisters so I can't imagine what it must be like. I'm close to my father though and couldn't imagine not having him around.'

'Is your father here with you today?' I assumed from the look of him that my new friend was also part of the blessing. He was tall with a handsome face and wore a floor-length navy overcoat with a small white collar and a cross hanging around his neck.

The young man nodded in the direction of the top table and pointed at the holy man sitting to the lord's right. The boy's attire made more sense now.

'My father is performing the blessing today. He's extra excited because it's my coming of age too.'

'So, you live in the city?' It was a redundant question as I already knew the answer but talking to anyone outside of the Link felt alien to me.

He didn't seem to notice my discomfort and happily rambled on about growing up within the walls, picking apples for the cook, and helping his father with his duties.

He managed to manoeuvre me into a seat between him and a surly-looking parent who cast a dismissive glance my way before filling his plate with ham and bread.

'I'm Theo by the way.'

I'd zoned out of the chatter and gave Theo an apologetic smile.

'I'm Marianne, or Maz to my friends, and my brother is Noah, but we call him Newt.'

'It's lovely to meet you, Maz.' He extended his hand, and I took it, shaking firmly just as my father had taught me.

Whether it was the gentle buzz of conversation or the delicious smells from the feast, I didn't know, but for the first time in a long while, stirrings of contentment arose in me. Newt was safe, his belly full, and I was making friends. Maybe today was going to be a good day after all.

The food and sweet treats continued to flow for several hours as the laughter and conversations infused the cloying air. Guards stood to attention along each wall of the great hall, their presence a constant reminder to me that I wasn't home, I wasn't safe, and I wasn't as welcome as Theo assured me I was.

Several of the guests around the tables were watching us and whispering amongst themselves. I tried to ignore them, but it was difficult.

'Don't pay any attention to them,' Theo said, bumping his shoulder against mine. 'They've never seen such a pretty girl before, that's all.'

I laughed at his words. 'You're probably the nicest person I've ever met, Theo.'

He scowled for the first time. 'Aren't your friends in the Link nice to you?'

My mind wandered briefly to Robbie, and I rolled my eyes. 'Most definitely not!'

'Perhaps you should think about moving into the city then.' He winked, and I slapped him playfully on the arm. Our conversations over the feast had centred on how out of place I felt, how stuffy the city folk were (present company excluded), and how soon the entire thing would be over so I could go home.

Before I could respond, an army of servants surged forward to clear away the empty plates. They descended on the great hall like ants, picking up and carrying off anything they could. It was mesmerising to watch.

Once the last servant had left, the dancers entered, circling through the hall, swirling long, brightly coloured sashes in the air. They resembled the travelling circus that came to the Link each winter. An explosion of colour and noise that moved as one and took you on a visual journey from the comfort of your seat. Each dancer held a single sash, which had a name woven into it, and as they came to a halt in front of the lord's table, I recognised the serious part of the blessing ceremony had begun.

One by one Crawford Reign called up the members of the blessing. Theo was first, clearly getting extra-special treatment for being the holy man's son. His sash was a deep navy with gold trim and matching writing, and as the dancer fastened it across Theo's chest he turned to grin at me.

I was flushed from the good food and the sneaky goblets of wine that Theo had managed to obtain for each of us. My head swam a little as I smiled back at him. Adjusting my gaze, I noticed Crawford Reign watching me. His face was slightly obscured by the floral display that decorated the top table, but I couldn't escape the intensity of his stare. He never flinched or altered his view but merely tilted his head in a curt nod. I blushed and twisted the fabric of my dress between my hands. The last thing I wanted was to mess up in front of the lord because I'd got a bit carried away with the wine.

Someone called my name and I took a deep breath. All I had to do was make it up to the front of the hall, be presented with my sash, and then it would all be over.

The walk to where Theo's father stood at the front of the room seemed to stretch on forever. All eyes focused on me. Whispers floated across the hall, and I flinched when one of the blessing girls murmured, 'Dirty Link rat.' I had never wanted to be at home in my small broken hut more than at that exact moment.

'Marianne Fitz, you have reached the age of maturity and can now honour your lord by contributing to the safety of this city and its people.'

I bit down on my tongue to stop from asking if the people of the lower towns, the plains and the mountain regions were included in this blessing.

'We celebrate your coming of age with a sash to remind you of your oath to your lord and duty to keep the peace.'

Theo's father placed his hand on my head and muttered something unintelligible before smiling down at me. His eyes crinkled at the sides and there was a warmth in his touch that calmed my nerves. Being so close to the holy man, I understood where Theo's positivity came from. Nobody could deny that they were father and son.

One of the flamboyantly dressed dancers advanced clutching a purple sash with my name embroidered in silver thread. I rounded my shoulders and lifted my chin in readiness to receive the final stage of the blessing. Before the dancer reached me, Crawford Reign called a halt to the proceedings. He circled the table and walked across to where I stood with Theo's father.

All the air left my body as I questioned how I could have offended the Lord of Obanac. From this position, I couldn't see Newt and wondered if perhaps he'd done something.

Crawford waved his hand dismissing the dancer and relieving her of the sash.

I bit down a little harder on my tongue as he stepped closer, pressing the palms of my hands tight to my sides to try to stop them trembling, but nothing could stop the swirling mass that churned my insides. What was he doing?

The lord slipped the purple sash over my head and circled behind me to fasten the clasp. He brushed my long red hair to the side, and my skin crawled at his touch. He was so close that I could smell the wine on his breath and the flowery scent of soap on his skin.

The silence in the room was tangible and I tried to keep my focus on the large tapestries decorating the wall ahead of me.

'There now, you're all done.' Crawford Reign smiled down at me, and I shuddered at the lack of light in his eyes. The great hall remained silent. Nobody dared make a sound as they watched their lord and the girl from the Link.

'Thank you, my lord,' I whispered before taking a step backwards to fall in line with the others.

I sneaked a look at Theo and gave him a half smile. The concerned look on his face didn't sit well with me, and I prayed that the stupid blessing would be over soon and I could grab Newt and run back to the safety of our home.

With the sashes handed out and the feast complete many of the guests began to make their way home. I weaved through the remaining visitors toward Newt's table where he now sat alone.

I was about to call out for my brother when Theo popped up in front of me with a wide grin.

'Just wanted to say goodbye before you left.'

I smiled back at him, but became distracted when one of the guards, the one we'd met earlier with the scar down his cheek, approached Newt. Over Theo's shoulder I kept a watchful eye on my brother, eager to get to his side but not wanting to appear rude in front of my new friend.

'Yes, thank you, Theo. If it weren't for you, I wouldn't have made it through this day.'

The guard was showing Newt his sword, and I cursed under my breath.

'Of course you would. You've got an inner strength that I don't think you even realise you possess, Maz.'

I dropped my head as the heat crept up my cheeks. I wasn't used to receiving compliments.

'Thank you, that's a lovely thing to say.' I thrust my hand out, which Theo took, but instead of shaking it he turned it over and kissed the top.

'Stay in touch, Maz.' Then he was gone, melting into the receding crowds.

I turned my attention to Newt and saw that the guard had left and my brother was now alone tossing a shiny red apple between the palms of his hand and waiting patiently for me.

I hurried to his side and ruffled his hair.

'Look what the guard gave me,' he said, the dimples in his cheeks prominent in his wide smile.

'Lucky boy. Are you going to eat it now?'

'No, I'm going to save it and show my friends. They'll be so jealous.'

I giggled at the excitement in his voice.

'Let's go home then, shall we.'

''Bout time!' he replied, jumping up from his seat and pulling me to the door.

We strolled out into the early evening sunshine and backtracked our way through the impressive gardens. I pointed out the various herbs on the way, teaching Newt which healed and which harmed.

The cobblestones still sparkled under the last few rays of the sun as we followed the path back to the main gate. Everything was so clean and fresh, from the floors to the buildings, even the people enjoying a pleasant stroll; everything was perfect, a sharp contrast to the living conditions out in the Link.

Keeping the castle on our right and the orchard on our left we navigated our way back to the portcullis with ease. Through the open gate I could see the bridge over the moat to the guardhouse and the track leading up to the iron gates in the distance. Beyond that was home.

I began to relax as we drew up to the gate. Two guards stepped forward and I smiled in greeting, but received a frosty glare in return.

'What have you got there, boy?' The guard drew his sword and snatched at Newt's arm.

I instinctively pulled my brother behind me.

'What are you doing? We've come from the blessing as guests of Crawford Reign, and now it's time for us to go home.'

'You can leave, but the boy isn't going anywhere.'

'Why!'

Panic flooded my chest as the guards circled us.

'He's stolen from the lord's orchard, and that's against the law.'

I half laughed in relief. 'No, you're mistaken. The lord's guard gave him the apple just before we left.'

'That's a lie. Nobody is allowed the apples. The workers pick them, and the cooks bake them, and as this little squirt is neither a worker nor a cook, then he must be a thief.'

The taller of the guards grabbed Newt and pulled him out of my reach. Wrapping a muscular arm around my brother's waist, he hoisted him off his feet and dragged him away.

I screamed in protest thrashing out at the other guard with my hands and feet.

'No! He's not a thief. Give him back to me.'

'Go home, girl; there's nothing you can do for him now.'

'There's been a mistake,' I cried. 'Ask the Lord of Obanac, he'll confirm it.'

The guard grabbed a handful of my dress and pulled me so close I could smell the ale on his breath.

'Do yourself a favour and forget you ever had a brother.'

He tossed me to the side like a discarded cape and marched off after the other guard. Newt's soft cries carried across the sky as the light failed and the stars began to appear. I trembled and sobbed as the guards disappeared from view with my brother, the city dwellers looking the other way.

All my fears were being realised, and as the sun slid behind the city walls, a deep chill settled in my bones.

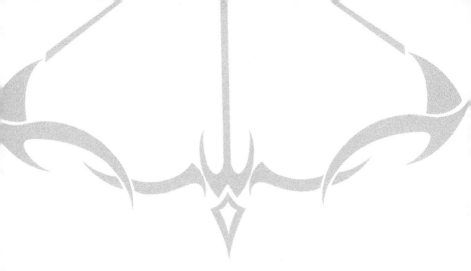

THREE

'It's an outrage! That young lad has done nothing wrong. We have to do something about it.' Mrs Elrod stood at the front of the communal hall where all Link business took place with her hands on her plump hips and a scowl on her wrinkled face.

The commotion I caused upon my return pulled the villagers of the Link from their homes. They huddled into the wooden building to hear how the guards dragged my brother from my arms. They shook their heads with pity as I sobbed into Mrs Elrod's shoulder, and they whispered about a loss of hope and forgotten families. Dread cloaked the faces of all the old folk as they reprimanded any of the youngsters who dared to show anger and defiance.

Mage Hall stood and addressed the room. 'We believe that young Newt is innocent, Mrs Elrod, but what can we do? We've got no power to argue with the guards, and no authority to influence the lord. Our hands are tied.'

'Poppycock! You're all scared of standing up for yourselves. Where's that spark that got us through the darkest days of the phantom's curse?'

'We were just children back then, Judy,' the man said softly. 'We've come such a long way since those days. Our families are safe living near the wards of the city. We need the lord's protection, and we don't want to risk upsetting the balance.'

'Nonsense. If black magic torched this earth again none of us would survive.'

'I want to help!' A dark-haired boy about twelve years old rose from his chair holding his hand in the air as if volunteering. His mother dragged him back into his seat, panic pinching at the creases in her face.

'Thank you, young Samuel. You're a brave lad, but your mam's right to stop you. The likes of you and Newt are the future of our community, and we need to keep you safe. It's your parents I'm urging to offer some aid.'

Mrs Elrod shuffled around the room eyeballing each person. The men hung their heads, and the women shrugged their shoulders. The fear in the room was palpable. Standing up to Crawford Reign and his soldiers was unthinkable to them.

'Tsk, you disappoint me. Not one of you is willing to help that lad then?'

The gathered party mumbled incoherently and avoided direct eye contact with Mrs Elrod. I swiped at my constant stream of tears before glancing around the room at the sea of lowered heads and broken people. What had happened to us? Where was that community spirit?

Rising from my seat, I crossed the space until I was standing next to my old friend. I placed a shaky hand on her arm to calm her anger and then addressed my friends gathered in the hall.

'I understand that you're scared of losing the lord's protection. I know that without Crawford Reign and the elite guard our homes and land could be lost, but all I ask is for one person to stand up and be a spokesperson for his release.'

'They don't release anyone from the Link who goes into those cells, Marianne,' Mage Hall said from his position at the front of the hall. The crowds nodded in confirmation. 'I'm truly sorry, but your brother is lost.'

I thought the tears might begin to flow again at his words, but instead a strange fire ignited in the pit of my stomach. I knew what he said was true, but I refused to believe that Crawford Reign was so wicked that he would condemn a young boy.

'I'll get my brother back with or without your help,' I said to the assembled townsfolk, clenching my teeth as I spoke.

The fire within me continued to rage out of control, sending tiny vibrations dancing along my arms and into my fingers, but it was matched by the terrible ache in my chest, which was growing in size as my neighbours and friends turned their faces away from me.

'I'll help you any way I can, lass,' said Mrs Elrod.

I reached for my friend's hand and squeezed her fingers. In unison, we both turned to leave. A few of the assembled villagers called out warnings, but we kept walking. The people were afraid, but I needed to stay strong for my brother, and for myself. I didn't want to be surrounded by the weak-minded.

'I'll go to Crawford Reign myself,' I said as we pushed open the doors and spilt out into the town square. The market stalls were closed for the night, and the only sounds were the concerned murmurings of the people in the building behind us.

'Is that a wise move, Maz? We don't know if we can trust him.'

'It's the only thing I can do, Mrs E.'

She grabbed onto my hands and pulled me closer.

'Then that's the plan. First thing tomorrow you'll seek out Crawford Reign, and if he doesn't listen, then we'll go with plan B.'

I frowned.

'What's plan B?'

'If the lord isn't willing to release Newt, then we'll find a boy willing to rescue him. We'll travel to the plains and speak to Robbie.'

I closed my eyes and took a deep breath in.

'I don't think Robbie will want to help after what he said to me before the blessing. He thinks I've abandoned the people out there on the plains.'

'He knows deep down that you'd never abandon anyone. He might be a bit stroppy at first to save face, but you'll talk him around. He's a troublesome lad but his heart's in the right place.'

I wasn't convinced, but Mrs Elrod refused to think that Robbie would turn us away.

'He might be a fool at times, but he's brave and strong, and I know he'll want to help Newt,' she said.

'I hope so. Maybe all he needs in life is a purpose.'

'Well, we can certainly give him one of those.' She chuckled. 'Now, get some sleep, lass, you'll need your strength for what's to come.'

The serving girl who had collected me from the gatehouse led me into a small courtyard full of bulbous flowers in every possible shade of blue. She pointed to a bench and told me to wait. I sat down and breathed in the intoxicating scent of the blooms.

The courtyard was like an oasis in a sea of stone, and the sun beat down on the small area giving it a welcoming feel. My request to meet with Crawford Reign was accepted within minutes of my arrival at the gatehouse, and I was told I would meet him in his private chambers.

My stomach rolled as I tried to calm my breathing and focus my mind on my mission. I was willing to beg the lord on my hands and knees if it meant getting my brother back.

'Marianne, how lovely to see you again.'

My eyes flew open, and I jumped to my feet at the sound of his voice. He was leaning against the doorframe wearing black trousers and a loose robe that hung open. I tried not to look at the muscles on his torso.

'Thank you for seeing me at such short notice, my lord.'

'Not at all. I was hoping I'd get to see you again.'

His comment confused me. Only yesterday he was warning us to stay away from the family silver in his not-so-moving speech, and now he was pleased that I was standing in front of him. Before I could give it more consideration he had cleared the court- yard and was by my side. He took my hand and kissed the top of it, his stubble tickling the skin. Every fibre of my being wanted to shy away, but instinct told me to hold steady.

'As wonderful as it is to see you again too, my lord, I'm afraid I'm here on business.'

He released my hand and studied me with an amused expres- sion.

'What business is it you want to discuss?'

I took a deep breath and launched into the events of the pre- vious evening. Crawford listened and nodded at all the right plac- es. His brow furrowed as I relayed what the guard had said to me about forgetting I had a brother, but he didn't interrupt, and I dared to hope that he was genuinely concerned.

'It's a simple misunderstanding that can be cleared up with your help, my lord. I'm begging you to release my brother and let me take him home.' I felt emotionally and physically drained as I waited for an answer.

The lord studied me for a moment longer and then invited me to sit beside him on the sun-drenched bench.

'Nothing would give me greater pleasure than to return your brother to you. However, I can't be seen to show favour to any of the prisoners. There must be a trial, as is the law, Marianne.'

A single tear ran down my cheek. Could I argue with the Lord of Obanac and not be reprimanded? Would it do us any good?

'I understand that you must follow the rules, my lord, but a grievous mistake has been made and your guard can attest to that without any need for a trial.'

'Do you know the name of this guard?'

I shook my head. 'No, but he has a long scar down his face.'

'Plenty of my guards have scars, Marianne. That's a fact of life if you're a soldier.'

Was it me or was Crawford Reign being intentionally difficult?

'I'm sure you'd realise who he was if you saw him,' I said in my attempt to convince him of Newt's innocence. 'We could go and find him.'

'You want me to find one soldier in a battalion! No, I'm sorry, Marianne, the law is clear and my hands are tied.'

If I uttered another word I knew I would break down, so I stood, nodded at the lord, and turned to leave.

'Wait!' he said, grabbing my elbow to prevent me from going. 'There might be one way I can help.'

Hope flared in my chest.

'I'll release your brother if *you* stay in Obanac, in my household.'

I blinked. Was he serious?

'You want me to be your servant?'

'I want you to stay in the city.'

'As a servant?'

'Not necessarily. You could be my permanent guest. I could do with some female company to lighten the dull days of endless meetings with old men who smell of rotting feet.' He huffed at his own joke but my gut rolled at the thought of being his female companion.

'With respect, my lord, I'm a bit young to be anybody's *companion*.'

Crawford chuckled but the sound sent a trickle of ice running down my spine.

'I meant it as a token gesture for the city. I know the people would like to see a lady within the walls again even if it's only as a loyal friend.' He took my hand in his and I fought the instinct to pull free. 'I want you to stay in the city with me, Marianne. I find you enchanting and strong-willed and I'd like to get to know you better. We can work out the details later, but if you agree, then I can have your brother returned to the Link today.'

'What if I agree to stay in Obanac if my brother can stay with me too?'

Crawford bristled and began fiddling with the hem of his shirt.

'I'm afraid that's not possible, Marianne. Once a crime has been committed then that prisoner, even if found not guilty during the trial, must be banished from the city. Your brother would be released but he couldn't have anything to do with you once you were Lady of Obanac.'

'No!' I pulled my hand free, my heart pounding in my chest, but I couldn't stop the words that poured from my lips. 'I'm not a lady; I'm a healer from the Link who gets her hands dirty on the blood of your people. Our home might not be as grand as those in Obanac, but it's ours. I love my faded curtains and open fire, and I never want to leave that behind. I was born there, and so was Newt. I could never leave the Link and I would never leave my brother behind.'

My shoulders lifted slightly as I faked confidence I didn't feel. I was either about to be laughed at, banished, or beheaded.

'Then your brother remains in his cell.'

'Why are you doing this?' I cried, despair in my voice as I realised there was nothing else I could do.

'I want you, Marianne, and I always get what I want.'

It was obvious I wasn't going to win but I needed to make it crystal clear to the Lord of Obanac that I wasn't his to command. I lifted my chin and squared my shoulders to demonstrate how pigheaded I could be. Maybe he would see my obstinate behaviour and change his mind, releasing my brother in the process and banishing the pair of us from Obanac.

Instead, he stormed out, muttering under his breath and giving me time to run for the gatehouse. I wanted to get as far away from Crawford Reign as possible.

I didn't know why he'd chosen me, or why he needed me to stay in the city so badly.

My younger self would have giggled, blushed, and planned her new adventure in the city, but this Marianne, the one who had seen her parents torn from her grasp, had cleaned up the blood of her people, and who sensed that Crawford Reign was not what he seemed, she wanted to run for the hills at his offer.

The walk back to the Link seemed to take forever. I'd promised to report to Mrs Elrod upon my return but now I understood that without the lord's help I was facing Mrs E's plan B, which meant seeking out Robbie and convincing him to help me rescue my brother before a sulking Lord of Obanac decided to harm Newt because of my rejection.

Why did it feel like I'd escaped the scorpion's tail only to be facing the dragon's fire?

The sun's rays were high in the sky when we set off for the plains. Samuel, the brave young boy from the previous night who stood up and offered his help when all the adults turned their backs, met us outside the community building with an old horse and rickety cart.

'I wish I could come with you to help Newt,' he said, his eyes shining with unshed tears. It was only now I recognised him as one of the boys Newt liked to spend time with.

'My dad's going to give me a whipping for stealing his horse and cart, but I couldn't stay at home and do nothing. I want you to take it.'

'Thank you, Samuel.' I was deeply touched by his kind act and only wished more of my neighbours could be so considerate. 'We'll bring Newt, and your horse, back home safe and sound.'

Samuel giggled and handed me the reins. His small chest puffed with pride as he smiled up at me.

'Good luck, Maz.' With that he shot off between the shacks, no doubt looking for a suitable hiding place from his father.

Mrs Elrod pulled herself up onto the cart and slung her bundle of supplies in the back.

'Let's go then,' she said with a slight twinkle in her eye.

If Mrs E had been looking for adventure, then she'd got it, and yet a strange lightness filled my chest as we trundled out of the Link and along the main dirt road in the direction of the plains. I'd spent my entire life in that tiny shack in the Link, as had my parents, and to be leaving my routine, and the relative safety of my community, caused my head to ache and my palms to sweat, but I couldn't shake that feeling of rightness at what I was doing. Since the phantom's black magic had torn through the lands, nobody dared to question what had become normal to us, except for Robbie.

My thoughts moved to the young man we sought. There was no denying that he was handsome and made my stomach lurch alarmingly, but Robbie challenged that routine I was so used to. He rebelled against the rules laid down by the lord's advisors and refused to live by any other standards than those he set for himself. Being in his world might be just what I needed to find the power to save my brother. The outlaw could be our only hope.

We travelled until the sun began its descent in the sky, neither of us talking. The trees had grown sparser as the journey continued. Lush green grass gave way to scorched earth. The track we followed jostled the cart enough to rattle our teeth, and it was getting more and more difficult for me to manoeuvre the rocks and craters. Not many people journeyed this far away from the protection of the city, and very few wanted to witness the destruction that had befallen the land.

The road came to an abrupt halt as the plains stretched out ahead of us, butting up to the mountains on the horizon.

'I think we'll be walking from here, Mrs E.' I jumped from the cart and helped my friend down. Unhooking the cart from the horse, I coaxed it along the dusty terrain toward a plume of smoke in the distance.

'Do you think he'll help us?' I asked, keeping my eyes on the horizon as we picked our way over the boulders and dead trees.

'I hope so, lass. Robbie looks out for the folk on the plains and God knows they don't have it easy, and just like them he's a good person, and he knows right from wrong. It's a pity the Link folk can't muster enough fire in their bellies to join us.'

I grunted my agreement and tugged on the horse's reins.

I'd never ventured this far out onto the plains before, and within half an hour we had reached the outskirts of a small village. I scoured the dirty faces searching for Robbie, Fergus, or Xander. Children wearing rags ran to us with nothing on their feet to protect them from the sharp rocks. Mrs Elrod pulled a loaf of bread from her pack and handed it to the wide-eyed following. They squealed with delight and shot off across the dusty expanse of land to hide behind a blackened tree trunk with their prize.

Others arrived to watch us pick our way through the village. I laughed to myself at the use of the word *village*. There were no wooden shacks for shelter here. Families lived beneath animal skins anchored to rocks, exposed to the weather and wild animals that roamed the area.

'Judy! How lovely to see you again, how can we help you?' a man with a thick head of grey hair shouted out as we approached a large firepit.

'Hello, Ely, we're looking for young Robbie. The lass here needs his help.'

'He's hunting in the forest,' another voice shouted as several arms lifted to point in the direction of the mountains.

'Of course he is,' mumbled Mrs Elrod.

'We've got to go in there?' I inclined my head toward the tightly woven brambles that threaded their way through the lush vegetation creeping up the side of the mountain. A path that seemed unfit for human traffic. 'How does anyone get in there?'

'Hmm, looks like some people do. If you want to find Robbie, then you'll have to find a way through to the forest.'

'Me! Why aren't you coming?'

'That cart has rattled these old bones enough, lass; I need to rest my feet. Besides, Robbie won't want to see me. It's you that's got to convince him to help.'

I knew this was my mission and that my old friend had been kind enough to accompany me this far, but it didn't help quench the nausea that raged inside my gut at the thought of going into the forest alone.

'Come on, lass; I'll walk you to the edge. Oh, and you'll probably be needing this to hack your way through.' She handed me a long-handled sword, which I took, resigned to my mission. I just hoped Robbie didn't laugh in my face when I eventually found him.

Mrs Elrod led the way as she handed out vegetables and bread from her pack to the residents of the plains. Grateful faces surrounded us as we steered through the evergrowing crowds.

A deep rumble in the distance halted our advance. The faces which only seconds ago had shown gratitude were now etched with fear and dread. Grubby hands pulled at our sleeves urging us to run. I looked around in a panic as the floor trembled like a monster was stirring beneath the surface. Children scattered in all directions as the adults shouted out in alarm.

'What's going on?' I cried, watching the chaos unfold before my eyes.

'Run for your lives!' Ely shouted as he grabbed Mrs Elrod by the elbow and propelled her toward the tree line.

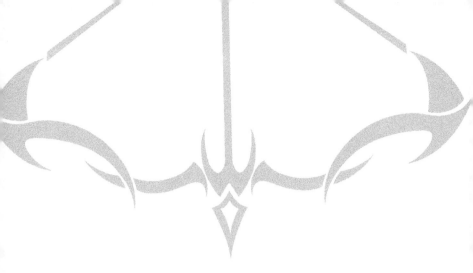

FOUR

The earth trembled as the beasts' hooves pounded the dirt carving up the land and leaving a cloud of dust in their wake. The Black Riders descended like a swarm of locusts coating the lands. Their silver blades sliced through the air hacking down anyone who got in their way.

The riders never ceased; pushing their charges forward they tore up the village, trampling women and children underfoot and butchering the men. The once parched land of the plains now soaked up the blood that flowed like a piglet suckling milk from its mother's teat.

I screamed out a warning to Robbie, who was running across the barren land as fast as his limbs could carry him, urging Fergus and Xander on, adrenaline powering their muscular frames as they scrambled over boulders and dodged the blades wielded by the Black Riders. Sweat covered their faces and soaked their tunics.

Robbie was shouting at his friends over the din, swerving the horseman who bore down on his position.

Despite the brightness of the sun, there was no shine to the rider's black helmet; it was like the energy from the burning star had been absorbed by a swirling mass of black fog.

One of the demons raised the sword in his hand to strike and I watched Robbie tuck his chin into his chest and roll forward manoeuvring out of the blade's arc. The rider thundered past him, his black eyes finding another target. A scream filled the air, and I spun in time to see the village mage sliced in two.

On the horizon, a lone hooded figure sat on horseback watching the bloodshed. With a flick of his wrist, he nudged his horse forward until he melted away into the haze of the setting sun. The Black Riders ceased their sport as if pulled from the carnage by an unseen tether. They circled the village once more, dragging two young girls onto the back of their horses, and faded into the distance, following the mysterious hooded horseman, their murderous mission complete.

The boys were panting in the dirt, huddled beside the rocks that marked the foot of the mountains. The coppery smell of blood tainted the air.

Slowly the survivors began to inch out from the smoke and debris. People wept as they crouched over their dead, and children sobbed at the sight of their ruined village.

I wiped the sweat from my face as the images of death steamrolled through my mind.

'Your mage is dead,' I said to nobody in particular.

Mrs Elrod burst from the trees, rushing to the mage's corpse. She knelt by the body muttering a prayer before jumping up and moving to the next.

I was numb all over. The shock of what I'd just witnessed had overloaded my senses. It was one thing to be called upon to offer healing to the wounded, but another thing altogether to witness the devastation and carnage firsthand. I picked up a smouldering animal skin and beat it until the tiny flames extinguished. It didn't feel like much but to these people that skin was a roof over their family's head.

Like in a dream I moved through the remains trying to salvage as much as possible. Nobody stopped me or asked me what I was doing. Everyone was doing whatever they could to help.

Mrs Elrod and Ely were tending to a woman with a deep gash along her arm.

'It's the third time in as many moons that the Black Riders have come,' Ely said, a slight tremor to his voice. 'It's sport for them.'

'Can't you go somewhere safe?' Mrs Elrod asked.

'Where would we go, Judy? They'd find us no matter what we did, or where we went. Poor Mage Leigh set up wards around all the villages as best he could, but they always find a way through. They want to finish what the phantom's black magic started and cleanse the lands of everyone but those who bow to the lord's rule.'

I was about to ask him what he meant when loud voices filled the air behind us. I whirled around in time to see Robbie and Fergus rushing toward them with Xander bringing up the rear, their swords and daggers drawn.

Since Robbie headed straight for Ely, who was still kneeling at my feet, I assumed he must be the village elder and took a step back to give them room.

'What the hell happened to the wards, Ely?' Robbie shouted.

'They must have found a way to drop them,' he replied. 'And they killed our mage.'

The muscle in Robbie's cheek twitched as he surveyed the scenes around him. Bodies lay scattered, their blood soaking into the parched earth. He nodded at the survivors as if congratulating them on staying alive, and as his inspection swept across the plains his eyes found mine.

'What are *you* doing here?'

I shuffled on the spot unable to find my voice. I didn't know if I'd ever be able to speak again or whether if I opened my mouth nothing but a piercing scream would come out. The silence stretched on and on until I was almost too embarrassed to answer him.

'She needs your help, lad.' Mrs Elrod came to the rescue.

Robbie looked at the old woman in disbelief before striding up to me, his nose inches from mine.

'What on earth could the Lady of the Link need my help with?'

I flinched at the sarcasm in his voice. I knew we had a strained relationship (at best) but I couldn't really call it a relationship. He tried to steer Newt into dangerous activities, and I reprimanded him for it. After our last conversation, I was surprised he was speaking to me at all, especially now I'd witnessed for myself the aftermath of an attack.

'It's Newt,' I managed to mutter. 'The lord's men took him.'

He stepped back and had the good grace to look shocked. Fergus and Xander approached, flanking Robbie like they were his bodyguards.

'What the hell does Crawford Reign want with your kid brother?' Fergus asked.

'I don't know.' It might not be a wise move to admit that the Lord of Obanac wanted *me* in exchange for Newt. I was fairly certain that Robbie would agree to those terms and hand me over personally. 'We were at the blessing, and everything was going so well, but then a guard gave Newt an apple and the gatekeepers wouldn't let us leave. They said he stole it, but it was a lie.' A sob caught in the back of my throat and I covered my face with my hands. A warm arm circled my shoulders, and I half expected to see Mrs Elrod comforting me, but instead it was Xander, Robbie's strong and silent friend, who had stepped up to offer some solace.

'Don't worry, we'll get him back for you,' Xander said, his soft voice a sharp contrast to his large, muscular frame.

'What?' Robbie stepped forward again to talk directly to his friend. 'We don't owe *her* anything, and our people need us here.'

I could feel Xander bristle at Robbie's words, but he remained silent.

'I'm not asking you to help me,' I snapped. 'I'm asking you to help Newt. He worships you, Robbie. It doesn't matter how many times I tell him to stay away from you he always finds a way back into your world.'

Robbie chuckled, obviously remembering the many times Newt had joined them on their adventures.

'It doesn't change anything. You can see that the people need us here, and we can't be running off to help a little kid who stole an apple.'

'He didn't steal anything!' I shrugged Xander's arm from my shoulder and shoved Robbie in the chest with both hands, anger pumping through my veins. That sharp crackle of power shot through me once again.

He stumbled backwards with a look of surprise on his face. Not stopping to think it through, I grabbed a fallen branch from the floor and brandished it like a weapon, pointing it at Robbie.

Fergus and Xander exchanged an amused look but moved in unison to try to disarm me. Unfortunately for them, I was running on pure rage now. I sidestepped a lunge from Fergus, tapping him on the back with my log before sticking my foot out, causing him to fall flat on his face. Rounding on the gentle giant, I snarled at Xander, who glanced in Fergus's direction giving me the opportunity to swipe the tree limb in a wide arc and knock his feet out from under him. I watched with satisfaction as he fell heavily on his backside.

Robbie clapped his hands together slowly and bowed his head at me.

'Impressive, my lady,' he mocked.

'Go to hell,' I screamed, launching myself at him.

He dodged my attempts to wrap the branch around his head, knocking it from my hand with ease, but he couldn't escape the slap I administered with my free hand. His cheek shone bright red and tears filled his eyes. Not wanting to give him a moment to recover, I punched forward, striking him in the shoulder then spinning to elbow him in the gut. Robbie let out a gasp as he doubled over.

'Okay, okay,' he rasped. 'I give up! We'll help you get Newt back.'

The corner of my mouth twitched into a half smile as I looked down on the three boys. Two lay in the dirt silently cursing and Robbie was bent over double trying to catch his breath.

'Well done, lass,' Mrs Elrod said as she steered me away from the dusty, foul-mouthed boys. 'They won't underestimate you again.'

I chuckled behind my hand.

'You've got all the help you need now,' she continued. 'I'm going to stay behind and help Ely rebuild the village.'

'Of course. We'll head back to the Link in the morning. I just hope we're not too late to save my brother.'

'So, how do you know we can trust this preacher boy?' Robbie asked.

Robbie, Fergus, and Xander had travelled back across the plains with me at first light. We had taken much longer than I had hoped, following the trail of bodies left by the Black Riders before reaching the Link and returning Samuel's horse and cart and saving the young boy from a beating.

'Theo was kind to me at the blessing, and I think he'll help us.'

'That's it! Someone was kind to you and you automatically trust them?'

I glared across at Robbie as we worked our way through the shacks in the direction of my home. Most of the residents in the Link disappeared into their dwellings when they spotted the four of us, clearly still unwilling to offer help in rescuing Newt.

'Theo was the only person who spoke to me in the city, and when he did, he wasn't arrogant. He was genuine, and I believe in my heart we can trust him.'

'Okay, my lady, it's on your head if he turns out to be like all the rest of the city folk.'

I stopped abruptly, causing Fergus to crash into the back of me.

'Stop calling me my lady. I know you don't like me, Robbie, and I know I let you down by choosing to go to the blessing rather than helping the people out on the plains, but I hope you at least have enough compassion in your bones for my brother.'

Robbie crossed his arms over his chest and gave me his award-winning smile.

'Who said I didn't like you?'

I started walking again.

'It's pretty obvious! You make fun of me all the time, call me names, and you're always trying to lead my brother astray.'

Fergus laughed out loud, and the sudden sharpness of the noise made me jump.

'In Robbie's world that would mean you're one of his most trusted allies.'

I looked behind me in time to see Robbie thump his friend on the arm. They exchanged whispered insults and a series of tussles before Fergus rolled his eyes and admitted defeat.

'I don't dislike you, Maz,' Robbie continued, striding ahead of Fergus to catch me up. 'I don't really think about you at all if I'm honest.'

A vice tightened around my chest on hearing his words. I didn't know why his comment upset me so much, but I wasn't about to jeopardise Newt's safety because Robbie didn't care about me in a certain way.

'Fine, then let's just get on with saving Newt, shall we.'

I picked up the pace, giving myself some distance from the boys. My mind was racing with awful scenarios and a deep fear for my brother, and even though I desperately needed Robbie's help, I wanted more than anything to be on my own with my thoughts.

My home was exactly as I'd left it. The comb I'd used to brush Newt's hair ahead of the blessing sat on the upturned crate. My green dress and shoes lay abandoned in a heap where I'd changed back into my trousers and shirt before leaving for the plains. Nub ends of candles sat in ceramic pots waiting for darkness to fall.

I drew the tattered curtain across the door once all three boys were inside. Their energy spread throughout the small space, and the shack suddenly felt way too small. I gestured for them to sit and they all chose a spot on Newt's cot, huddled together like mischievous children. I sat on my own bed facing them and took out a piece of parchment and a quill and ink pot.

'I'll send Theo a note and see if he can come out to the Link and meet us.'

'How are you going to get the note to him?' Xander asked.

'There's a pedlar who visits the city daily; he was a good friend of my father and should deliver it for us. I'll slip out tonight and speak to him.'

I bent over the yellowing parchment and began crafting the letter to Theo. I hoped that he was everything I wanted him to be and would offer us some help.

'Now we wait,' Robbie mumbled as he lit the candles.

Dusk arrived and with it the realisation that Newt was spending his third night in a dark cell. My breath caught in my throat as I tried not to cry and I distracted myself by clearing the plates from our supper.

Robbie and I had been out hunting earlier, so we had meat for dinner, something I was grateful for as I hadn't appreciated how hungry I was until the smell of roasting rabbit invaded my nostrils. Holding my bow and arrow in my hands again felt natural and relaxed my jittery nerves for a time.

I carried the scraps out to the pigsty, recalling Robbie's words as we'd made our way back to the Link with supper.

'*Ever killed a man with your arrows?*' he'd asked.

I'd been aghast that he thought I would be capable of such a thing, but as my mind wandered to Newt curled up in a frightened ball in some dark cell, I realised I might be willing to use my bow and arrow to kill something other than my dinner.

Was I ready for that?

'*It changes you,*' Robbie had whispered, and I marvelled at how complex this handsome boy was. One second he infuriated me, and the next he shocked me with his sincerity.

He didn't go into details, and I didn't press him; instead, we walked in comfortable silence.

The boys had grabbed what blankets they could find and made themselves at home. Fergus was sprawled across Newt's cot snoring softly, and Xander had made himself a bed on the floor by the small stove. Robbie hovered by the window staring out at the night sky.

'There are some spare blankets in the chest,' I said, nodding to the wooden crate at the end of my bed.

Robbie acknowledged me but bypassed it to sit next to me. Wriggling out of his boots, he swung his legs up so we were both lying side by side in my small bed. I flinched slightly at his closeness, but he didn't appear to notice.

'Do you think he's scared?' Robbie asked, his voice soft as he watched the flickering light on the ceiling from the candle.

'I think he'll be terrified.'

'What possessed the lord to have him arrested in the first place? Did he say anything that could have offended him?'

'Nothing at all. He was so nervous that he didn't even open his mouth. Crawford Reign had nothing to do with us, and we gave him no cause to warrant an arrest.'

'Who knows what goes on in that boy's mind? There are whispers that he sacrifices young girls for dark magic, and that he was the one to kill his own father.'

'Robbie! You can't say things like that. If anyone heard you, you could be arrested and killed.'

He shifted on the bed so he was looking down at me.

'So, now you care about what happens to me,' he teased.

'I care about *all* the residents in the lower towns *and* on the plains, and I don't want anyone else getting hurt.'

'Let's hope none of us gets hurt saving young Newt then, eh?'

Robbie's words brought home just how dangerous the mission was that I had asked them to help me with. What if they did get hurt? What if we were too late and the guards had harmed Newt? I shivered and pulled my blanket higher under my chin. Even with Robbie's closeness the deep chill that surrounded me wouldn't leave.

Voices and the sounds of cartwheels stirred me from my dreams, and I opened my eyes slowly. My face was warm, and it took me a few seconds to realise I was resting on Robbie's chest, his steady heartbeat filling my senses. I jumped up, mortified to find my arm also slung around his waist and our legs entwined.

The heat rushed up my neck and across my cheeks as I reclaimed my limbs and leapt out of bed. Robbie watched me with a smile dancing at the corners of his mouth.

'Not a word!' I hissed.

A sharp knock on the wall caused me to yelp, waking Fergus and Xander.

The pedlar stood outside clutching a note with a blue wax seal.

'I delivered your note, and the young man was quick to respond. He even stuffed my belly with chicken and bread for my trouble.' He winked and handed me the parchment scroll. 'Hope it's good news.' With that, he disappeared down the track and back to the market square.

My hands shook as I looked down at the wax seal. A crow sat on a branch: the lord's seal. Had the pedlar delivered the note to the wrong person? Was the elite guard about to sweep through the Link burning and murdering my friends because of my actions?

'What does it say?' Fergus yawned and stretched, interrupting my muddled thoughts.

I perched on the edge of my bed breaking the seal as I unravelled the paper.

My dear Maz, I am so sorry to hear about your brother. If there is anything I can do to help you, then I am your servant. I'll be travelling to the main gates of the city with my father at noon as he performs his annual pilgrimage. If you can come, I will meet you there. Your friend Theo.

'Your servant! Blimey, you must have made a good impression on him.' Robbie read the note over my shoulder, and before I could chastise him, he had snatched the page and was pacing the floor reading it over and over.

'A pilgrimage, does that mean they'll have no soldiers with them?' Fergus asked.

'I doubt it,' said Robbie. 'The Lord of Obanac wouldn't let his faithful holy man go wandering the land without an escort.'

'So what's the plan?' Xander stood up and drew his sword.

'I'll meet him alone,' I said, my voice sounding much calmer than I felt.

'What if it's a trap? What if the soldiers see you and decide to haul you off to the cells with Newt? What if...?'

I held my hand up to stop Xander's babbling.

'I'll be safe. I can stick with the crowds and work my way to Theo, and with all the pomp and ceremony nobody will notice a simple village girl chatting harmlessly to the holy man's son.'

'I don't like it,' Fergus said. 'It sounds too easy.'

Robbie had remained silent as he listened to the exchange but the gleam in his eye told me he had a plan of his own.

'What do you think we should do, Robbie?'

'I think you're right; you should meet this holy man's son on your own. Fergus, Xander, and I can hide in plain sight with the crowds and be ready to step in if you get in trouble.'

'Thank you.' I was both amazed and relieved that Robbie acknowledged my plan was good. Perhaps he wasn't as pigheaded as I'd initially thought.

The Link was buzzing, the residents out in force to see the holy man leave for his pilgrimage. There were five carts laden with cured meats, bread, wine, and cloth ready to be transported to the villages between Obanac and the next big settlement of Keaney over one hundred miles away. For some, the holy man's journey would save lives, but for others, it was already too late, and his services would be needed to perform funeral rites. Times were hard for everyone living in the shadow of the phantom's curse, unless they were fortunate enough to bask in the safety of Crawford Reign's magical wards.

I pulled my hood up to disguise my fiery red hair and melted into the swarming crowds as they made for the main gate. The holy man stood on a small plinth addressing the residents of the Link, but his words were lost on me as I scoured the assembled faces for Theo.

Just as I was about to give up, I spotted him at the back of the entourage. He was wearing a blue robe with a cream belt and a ceremonial dagger. His hood partially covered his features so I couldn't see his face clearly. The same seal that adorned the note he had sent was sewn onto his clothes. It was different from the lord's seal, which was a crow holding a scroll in its beak. Theo's crest was a crow sitting on a branch.

I pushed through the crowds until I was almost alongside the holy man. Guards occupied the space between him and the city gate, but fortunately there was no sign of Crawford Reign.

Robbie, Fergus, and Xander were in the crowd somewhere watching my movements and getting ready to step in should anything go wrong. It filled me with a sense of hope that someone was looking out for me.

Theo spied me and smiled from beneath his hood before directing one of the guards who stood next to him to move closer to his father. It gave him enough space to reach the edges of the crowd and get swept up in the bustle. He mingled with the residents, shaking hands and exchanging pleasantries. It dawned on me that I wasn't the only one who seemed to trust Theo.

The crowd surged forward to get closer to the holy man, and Theo and I took the opportunity to slip down a side street until we were out of view of the guards.

'Thank you so much for agreeing to help me.' I flung myself at my friend, giving him a tight hug, which he reciprocated with a chuckle.

'It's my pleasure. When I heard what happened to your brother I was horrified.'

'Do you know if he's safe?'

Theo nodded and took my hands in his. 'After receiving your note, I visited the cells. The beauty of being the holy man's son is I get access to the prisoners so I can give them comfort.'

'Did you see Newt?'

'Yes, he's scared but okay. I sneaked in some bread before the guards made me leave.'

'That's so thoughtful, thank you.'

'Yes, so thoughtful, preacher boy.' Robbie appeared from out of nowhere with his sword drawn and pressed the tip to Theo's throat.

'Robbie! What are you doing?'

'We don't know if we can trust him, Maz, he could be here to entice you away so the soldiers can throw you in that cell with Newt.'

Theo's face was ashen as Robbie, Fergus, and Xander surrounded him.

'Oh, for goodness' sake, move back all of you.'

I pushed at Xander's hefty frame until he shifted back a few feet, then pulled on Fergus's arm until he did the same. Robbie still held his sword against Theo's neck, but after receiving one of my most withering looks, he lowered it but kept it drawn.

'I understand that you don't trust the city folk and therefore don't trust me,' said Theo, 'but I'm no fan of Crawford Reign.'

'What do you mean?' asked Robbie.

Theo looked around as he checked for eavesdroppers.

'I see and hear many strange things in the city. My father has always told me to turn the other cheek and concentrate my efforts on helping the city folk, but I can no longer ignore what I see.'

Robbie sheathed his sword and folded his arms over his chest before nodding for Theo to continue.

'I've seen many young girls in the city mysteriously disappear after their blessing ceremony. They just vanish.'

I was briefly reminded of the young girls snatched during the raid on the plains by the Black Riders.

'What's he doing with them?' I was shocked at Theo's revelation and couldn't help but recall Robbie's words from the previous evening about dark magic and sacrifices.

'I don't know, but the guards are leaking rumours that something evil lurks beneath the castle.'

'Evil!' Fergus pushed forward. 'What do you mean *evil*?'

'Some of the loyal guards who serve my father believe that Cassias the sorcerer still lives in the lower levels. Nobody has seen him since the death of Davis Reign, but that doesn't mean he left the city. If the rumours are to be believed, he still exists, and there's every possibility that the sorcerer and Crawford Reign are using dark magic and practising sacrificial offerings.'

'That's impossible,' Fergus interrupted. 'The city is surrounded by magical wards to keep it safe from dark magic.'

'Yes, but the wards were built by Cassias. What if he found a way to get around his own magic spell?'

My head was bursting as I processed the possibilities of what Theo was saying. If Cassias was still within the city walls and was meddling with dark magic, nobody was safe, and that included the people in the city, the Link, and out on the plains.

'If all this is true, I need to get my brother out of the castle as quickly as possible.'

'I agree, and I can help you with that. There are secret entrances dotted throughout the city. I know of one that leads directly to the cells, but it's quite dangerous to reach. There's a door in the lower walls that was built by Davis Reign as an escape route should he ever need to leave the castle without detection. You'll need to climb down into the crater at the outer limits to find it.'

'The outer limits! You mean the bone-crushing, limb-severing, jagged rocks that surround the castle and are impenetrable by man,' Fergus mocked.

Theo nodded. 'I'm sorry I don't have an easier option for you. Davis Reign and my father were great friends, and the lord shared many confidences, one of them included the whereabouts of his favourite secret exit. Once you get into the crater, you'll find a man-made path to take you directly to the door.'

'If it takes us to the cells won't it be guarded or locked?'

Theo shook his head. 'The doorway gets used quite often by some of the guards who smuggle in wine. They don't believe it needs to be locked or guarded because nobody knows it exists.'

'Thank you so much, Theo,' I said, giving my friend a tight hug.

'I'm always here for you, Maz.'

Robbie coughed but I ignored him; instead I guided Theo toward the main street.

'Will you be travelling with your father?'

'No, he wants me to stay behind. There are too many jobs to take care of and he trusts me to handle them in his absence.'

'Well, I'm glad that you'll be sticking around.'

He smiled before checking the street ahead.

'Be careful, Maz.'

'Always.' I waved him off then turned to face Robbie, Fergus, and Xander.

Robbie's grin was feral as he addressed our small group. 'It's time to storm the castle.'

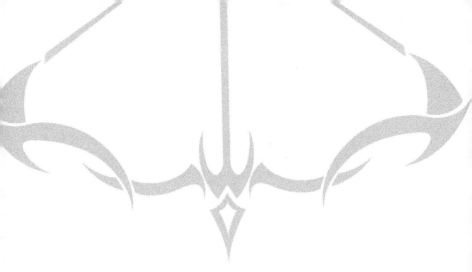

FIVE

The descent between the jagged rocks and choking vines surrounding the city was more perilous than I'd expected. When Davis Reign had fortified the area, it was with the intention of stopping anyone or anything from getting through the defences.

The rocks had been positioned like stalagmites raising up to the sky in mottled grey slivers. Some were filed to a point, and others relied on their natural form to create an obstacle for anyone stupid enough to attempt to penetrate their protection. Thick vines wound up and over the pillars creating a blanket of thorns and cover for the potential danger that lurked beneath.

I clung to the rope and dangled in mid-air while Robbie, Xander, and Fergus lowered my petite frame between the shards of polished stone. My thoughts drifted to my brother, who had been imprisoned for five nights now, and how every attempt to contact Crawford Reign had failed. Our plan was sound in theory, but to avoid suspicion, Theo suggested I continue my attempts to campaign for Newt's release.

Since returning from the plains I'd sent two letters to the young lord begging once more for him to free my brother. I was kidding myself if I ever hoped to appeal to his softer side—Crawford Reign didn't have one. He had said it himself, he wanted me, and he always got what he wanted.

I wondered once again why the Lord of Obanac needed me to stay in the city with him. He could have any girl he desired, and he was surrounded by beauty and grace every day, so why choose a girl from the Link?

My shin caught on the rocks and I winced. Glancing to the sky, I was grateful for the creamy glow of the full moon as it helped me not to feel quite so alone.

The strategy was a simple one. Lower me to the ground, let me find the hidden door, and I'd signal for the boys to follow. Having them to back me up was a comfort but also a distraction. When I hunted out in the woods I always went alone; I liked it that way. Time to process my jumbled thoughts, time to think about the what-ifs of life, and time to imagine what my days would be like if I was free to roam the lands hunting and healing without any responsibility. In my happy ever after my parents would find their way home from exile and we'd be reunited as a family once again.

A scraping sound dragged me from my musings, and I reached for the rocks to steady myself. In the crater below I spotted two guards hauling a wooden crate along what I could now recognise as a well-trodden path. I tugged on the rope, and my descent halted as the boys kept me suspended until the threat passed.

The guards were cursing under their breath as they lugged the box toward the main wall. As I mapped out their progress from above using the light of the moon, I could see the winding passage open up to a small courtyard within the rocks. Embedded into the wall was a small iron door, which stood ajar awaiting its cargo. I'd found our way in.

Swinging on the end of a rope above two armed guards was not how I'd expected my day to pan out. Their pace was slow-going for such muscular men, and I wondered what it was they were carrying that could cause them to exert that much energy.

A series of loud thumps emanated from the box and the guard to my right gave the wooden surface a hard kick.

'Shut it,' he growled.

The banging continued and was almost drowned out by the beating of my own heart in my chest. There was a person or people in that box.

I gasped, drawing the attention of one of the guards.

'Oi, what are you doing?'

He fumbled with his sword as they rounded on my position. Without thinking, I slipped my bow over my head and loaded an arrow. Using the rocks to brace myself, I shot one arrow before swiftly reloading and firing a second. Both guards dropped to the floor in a pool of blood.

I tugged on the rope once again with shaky hands and began to move lower and lower. I told myself over and over not to look at them as I untied myself from the rope even before my feet touched the ground. I ran to the crate trying not to disturb the guards' bodies. On the face of the box was an image of a crow holding a scroll in its beak—Crawford Reign's seal.

'Hello?' My voice shook. I wasn't even sure whatever was inside was human. I could have killed two guards to save a crate of chickens, but in my heart I knew something wasn't right.

Using my dagger, I broke open one of the panels and let it fall to the ground. In the darkness, I could see eyes shining out at me. Several pairs.

'It's okay,' I whispered. 'You're safe now.'

Three young girls crawled out of the box; their faces were bruised, their clothes dirty and tattered. They all had ropes around their necks, which were fastened to their bound hands. A wave of nausea washed over me as I set to work cutting their bonds and helping them to their feet.

'What, who, why...?' So many questions fought for space in my mind, but I had to offer these girls some semblance of control and focus if I was to get them to safety.

'Who are you?' I asked finally.

They huddled together, clutching each other close. The tallest of the three cleared her throat and spoke.

'I'm Helene; this is Ami and Tina. We were taken from our homes just after the blessing. They've kept us locked in a dark room ever since. We don't know where we are or why we're being punished. Today is the first time they've moved us.'

'The blessing?' I cast my mind back only a few days to the blessing I'd attended, and none of these girls were those who joined me when we received our sashes. 'Are you sure you're not mistaken?'

'No, I still had my sash on when they took me. I never had a chance to show my sister.'

Tears spilt down her filthy face, trailing lines in the grime.

'How old are you?'

Helene folded back in on herself and shrugged. 'Eighteen, I think.'

My hand flew to my mouth. Two years. These girls had celebrated their blessing two years ago. I turned my back on them so they couldn't see the panic on my face. Theo had suspected that something was going on but I had never for a second believed that the lord would be capable of something so wicked, and yet here was the proof—a crate with his seal, containing what I could only assume was a sacrificial offering, but an offering for what, or whom?

'Can you help us?' It was Ami who spoke now, her sunken cheeks and pale complexion making my heart ache.

'Of course,' I said. 'My friends are following me down here, and they'll be able to help me get you out.'

Right on cue, Xander appeared out of the darkness, startling the girls into faint screams. I calmed their nerves and threw Xander a withering look. He never noticed, his attention fully engaged on the sight in front of us.

'What happened to you?' he asked, more tenderly than you would expect from a boy his size.

Ami shrugged her tiny shoulders and wiped away the tears that fell in a constant stream. 'They gave us warm water and chunks of bread once a day but told us nothing of what was to become of us. We overheard bits of conversations between the guards but none of it made any sense to us.'

'What were they saying?'

'I heard them mention a name; Cassias, but other than that it was just routine guard chatter about keys, shift changes, and new prisoners.'

New prisoners. Newt. I was more desperate than ever to free my brother. While Theo had speculated that only girls were going missing, I didn't want to risk Newt's safety.

'Did they harm you?' Xander flexed his muscular arms as if readying himself to take on the entire elite guard single-handed.

Helene pointed to the bruise on her cheek. 'Only this because I asked too many questions when they were putting us into this crate.'

Robbie appeared out of nowhere, and I watched him assess everything around him. Within seconds he had no doubt calculated what had happened, what was going on at this precise moment, and what we should do next. His eyebrows rose upon seeing the fallen guards with my arrows protruding from their chests, and he gave me a fleeting glance before taking charge.

'We need to get you out of here before any more guards come in search of their friends,' he said, nodding at Helene to show he was here to help. 'Fergus is at the top waiting for us to return. Xander, can you take the girls back to the rope and help them navigate the rocks and vines while I go with Maz to get Newt?' He handed his friend a small dagger to cut through the choking greenery that blanketed the moat.

Methodical, focused, and professional. These were the thoughts rushing through my mind as I watched Robbie instruct Xander on how to manoeuvre the girls to safety. He was a natural leader, and yet I'd never seen this aspect of him before. He hid his sensible side behind the games and trickery, but I was starting to understand why Newt liked being in his presence.

'Ready to go?'

Robbie was standing in front of me now, his arm outstretched in the direction of the small iron doorway.

'Yes, of course.' I stumbled as I moved away, but he caught my arm to steady me.

'No rush, Newt's not going anywhere.'

He winked at me with a wide smile, white teeth flashing in the moonlight, and just like that he was back to being the mischievous Robbie I knew and loved to hate.

The iron door led to a dark passageway with minimal light cast from the single torch set into the stone wall. The constant drip, drip, drip of water grated on my nerves as we made our way to the end of the tunnel. In truth, we had no idea what we would find once the darkness spat us out. We were deep in the bowels of the city and finding our way up to the prison cells without being detected would be a miracle.

Robbie drew his sword the moment he set foot in the passage, ever ready for trouble should it jump out at us. I held my dagger in one sweaty palm and clung to my bow with the other. Nobody had mentioned the guards. Before leaving, Xander had stuffed their bodies inside the wooden crate and taken their weapons. He merely patted me on the back when we parted. The girls were too frightened to process what had happened, but Robbie clearly had an opinion, judging by his initial reaction.

'I had to kill those guards,' I whispered into the darkness.

'Uh-huh.'

'They would have sounded the alarm.'

'Uh-huh.'

'I had no choice!' I was aware that my voice had risen to a high squeak and my hands were shaking so much I nearly dropped my dagger.

Robbie halted in the corridor, and I walked straight into him with a grunt. He turned to look at me, his face partially lit up in the flickering firelight. His eyes were full of compassion, and my breath caught in my throat.

'You made a split-second decision, and it was the right thing to do,' he said, 'but killing someone changes you, inside. On the positive side I hope you didn't find it easy to kill the enemy. If you did, then I'd have something to worry about, but as it is I now know you're capable yet remorseful and that's the best sidekick anyone could hope for.'

He smiled and turned to resume his walk down the corridor.

'I'm not your sidekick, Robbie. This is my mission, and I'm allowing *you* to tag along for the ride.' I brushed past him so I could lead the way, fuming at his arrogance but secretly pleased to see the sparkle of admiration in his eyes. I wasn't going to let this outlaw think I was some damsel in distress. It was true that I needed their help, but if they'd turned their backs on me when we were on the plains, I would have carried on alone. I knew it and Robbie knew it.

We carried on in silence until we reached an inner chamber loaded with crates. For a terrifying moment I thought each one might be full of imprisoned girls, but upon closer inspection, it was just ale and grain.

'Over here.' Robbie was standing by a staircase. Lights and murmured conversations floated down to greet us. 'I think it's the guardhouse.'

He took the lead, and I was happy to follow this time. We crept up the stairs until we could see into the room. Only two guards were on duty at this time of night, and both of them were sitting with their backs to us warming themselves by the roaring fire that burned in the grate. Robbie gestured for me to go to the left where the wooden door to the prison cells stood open.

I hugged the wall as I tiptoed toward my prize. Newt was beyond this door, and I thought my heart might burst from my chest as I worried about my brother.

As I reached the door, my bow slipped from my shoulder and clattered to the floor. I tried to catch it but wasn't quick enough. Damn. Both guards jumped to their feet with a start. Their surprised expressions gave me time to think, and I smiled and bobbed my head.

'Evening, gentlemen, can I get you anything from the kitchens?' I was hoping to stall them from raising merry hell and setting every guard in the city on us.

They exchanged puzzled looks but didn't seem to see me as a threat; their shoulders relaxed as they considered my offer. Robbie loomed up behind them, and before they could ask me for chicken, bread, or ale they both felt the sharp sting of his blade.

Silently we pulled their corpses into a small alcove out of sight and rushed through to the cells, Robbie grabbing the keys from one of the guards' belts as we ran. The room was long and thin, stretching left and right, with chambers along the length of both walls. Sawdust covered the floor and a small torch flickered at either end of the space casting creepy shadows. Upon entering the cell block we split up in search of Newt. I hurried to the left as Robbie explored the cells on the right.

Solemn faces greeted me as I flew down the corridor. Old, young, men, and women, all thin and powerless. I wanted to free them all, but we didn't have the time or the skill for such a daring rescue. Newt was my priority.

'He's here,' Robbie hissed from the opposite end of the long room.

I ran to where he was crouching by the bars of a cage. Beyond the metalwork, a bundle of rags lay in a pile on the floor. It took me a while to realise the rags were, in fact, my brother. A loud sob caught in my throat.

'Newt?'

His shiny face looked up at me through the bars, and my heart shattered into a million pieces. He was pale and so very small. I didn't remember him being so small a few days ago. There were sores on his ankles and wrists where his rope bonds had chafed and his hair was matted.

The lock gave a loud click as Robbie turned the key and swung open the cage door. In one fluid motion, I was by Newt's side cradling my brother in my arms and sobbing gently into his hair.

'We need to move,' Robbie said, giving me a gentle nudge out of the way so he could scoop Newt up off the floor.

I led us back into the guardhouse and in the direction of the outer limits only to find a bewildered guard ascending the stairs and blocking our escape.

'Halt!' he shouted, pulling his sword from its sheath.

I shot another arrow, hitting the guard square in the chest. He dropped backwards, his sword striking the worn flagstones and clattering down the stairs. Raised voices and movement from the room above filled me with dread.

Robbie motioned to the alcove where we had stashed the other guards, and we melted into the darkness as six heavily armed guards burst into the room.

'You two check the prisoners, the rest of you with me.' The sergeant barked his orders before hurrying down the stairs toward the outer defences, and our friends.

Once they'd moved off, we stepped out of our hiding spot and sprinted up the stairs. Robbie had no trouble hoisting my frail brother in his arms.

We staggered out into the courthouse where the lord dealt his justice. The hall wasn't as grand as the one in the main house, but it was still impressive. High wooden ceilings with a lattice framework towered above us. Banners bearing the Lord of Oban-ac's coat of arms decorated the walls—the image of a crow holding a scroll in its beak, which I'd seen on a crate of prisoners. It made my blood run cold when I thought about it. Seating wrapped itself around the edges of the room where the city folk could come and watch justice being served. A raised wooden plinth dominated the end of the hall with a large throne-esque chair erected for the lord to use.

Heavy double doors led outside, and I knew from my recent visit that these would take us directly into the apple orchard and place us in full view of the city square and castle.

'We need to find another exit,' I whispered.

'What about this?' Robbie motioned to a servants' entrance hidden from view beneath one of the banners.

The blood was pumping through my veins so fast I could barely hear anything above the roar. A million what-ifs circled like vultures, but I knew our options were limited. We were in the city far away from our original escape route, and we needed to think and act quickly.

'Okay, go!'

The cool night air hit me in a rush, and I almost wept at the sweet smell of it. We were behind the courthouse looking at a series of streets that ran off from the main square. At first glance, I took them to be residential. As the clouds parted and the moon illuminated the sparkling cobbled paths, I caught sight of a lone building to our left, and my heart soared.

The majestic church stood like a beacon, surrounded by a neat lawn and flower borders, giving it the impression of being on its own island in the middle of the bustling city.

'There,' I said, pointing for Robbie's benefit. 'We'll find Theo, and maybe he can help us get out of here.'

We sprinted in the direction of the church as the cries of the guards filled the night air.

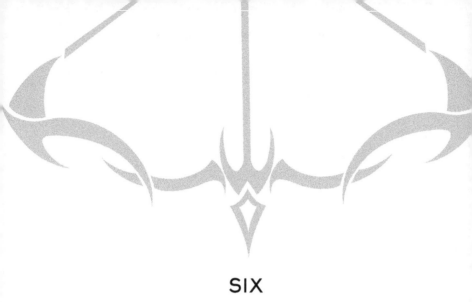

SIX

The door opened a fraction, and a sleepy pair of eyes peered out into the night. At the sight of me, Robbie, and Newt the door swung wide and Theo ushered us inside, his eyes darting to watch the dark streets.

He wore a plain woollen smock that swept the floor as he moved. It seemed odd without his collar, cross, and ceremonial belt, almost like a billowing nightgown, not the uniform of a holy man. His dark hair was sticking up in tufts where he had been sleeping on it, and I suppressed the urge to giggle.

'Sorry we woke you,' I said instead.

'It's fine. How can I help?'

He was wringing his hands and moving from foot to foot as he stayed close to the window so he could watch what was going on outside. We were in the main body of the church with its high ceilings and white walls. There were no flamboyant banners here only rows of wooden seats and a table with a crisp white cloth and a small vase of fresh flowers in the centre.

'We ran into trouble, and our escape route was compromised,' Robbie said, setting Newt down on the nearest pew.

I rushed to his side and checked my brother for any injuries. He grumbled as I prodded and poked.

'What can I do to help?' Theo asked, his voice slightly elevated.

'Are you okay?' I asked, leaving Newt in peace and approaching my friend. 'We wouldn't have come to you if we had any other choice. I know how dangerous this is for you.'

He smiled, his shoulders relaxing, and reached for my hand.

'It's fine,' he said again but this time with more confidence. 'My father is the one people call upon in difficult situations, and for a moment I realised he wasn't here to ask, but I'm sure we can figure a way out of this dilemma together.'

'Well, what would your father do with us?' Robbie asked, standing in the centre of the church with his arms folded and a deep frown creasing his brow. A sheen of sweat covered his face, and for the first time, I appreciated he was trying hard to stop himself from freaking out. It never occurred to me that we wouldn't get out of this predicament. Not until that precise moment.

Theo motioned for us to follow him through a door set into the back of the church, which led to the quaint living quarters. There was a single room with two small beds, a fireplace, a cooking pot, and a reading chair surrounded by piles of old books. Not what I expected from a dwelling in the city, and certainly not what I expected from the lord's holy man. I hadn't given it much thought until that moment, but I'd assumed Theo lived in one of the plush homes we'd walked past on the day of the blessing. Some of the owners had opened their doors to stand and wave as the procession ambled past and I'd taken the opportunity to look in at the splendour, the lavish furnishings, and shiny floor tiles within.

'You live here?' Newt said, his voice croaky. 'It reminds me of home.'

I chuckled as he flopped down onto the nearest cot and proceeded to curl up in a ball. Newt was right; it did resemble our modest hut. My heart ached as I thought about home. Would I even be able to return there or would the lord's guard tear it apart looking for Newt?

As if reading my mind, Theo took my hands in his and as gently as he could said, 'You can't take Newt back to the Link. That's the first place they'll look.'

'What do you suppose we do with him then?' Robbie was growing more unsettled with every second, and it made the butterflies in my gut feel like giant bats.

'Take him to the mountains,' he said. 'My friend Halia will keep him safe.'

'How is that going to help?' Robbie snapped. 'To reach the mountains we need to travel over the plains and the Black Riders are sweeping through and murdering anyone in the vicinity.'

'I don't think the Black Riders will be going out for a while.' Theo dropped my hands as he spoke and I had to believe I'd heard him wrong. How would the holy man's son know anything about the evil riders?

'What did you say?' Robbie spoke through clenched teeth and from the glint in his eye I expected him to draw his sword and run it through Theo's heart.

'I've been doing some more digging,' he said, squaring his shoulders so he stood at the same height as Robbie. 'There are strange things happening within the city walls. When I visited Newt in the cells, I overheard the guards talking about the army being kept close by in the city. They weren't talking about Crawford's elite guard or the city watch. They also talked about an important shipment from the dungeon, and I assumed this had something to do with the missing girls.'

Robbie put his hand up to stop Theo.

'We're way ahead of you on that one. The shipment you speak of, we found it, rescued it, and neutralised the guard involved with it.' His gaze flicked in my direction.

'So, it was the girls?'

'Yes, three of them,' I cut in. 'They've been held against their will for two years.'

Theo began to pace, scratching his head as he moved. I had an overwhelming urge to reach out and smooth his wayward hair.

'What of the Black Riders?' Robbie pressed. 'Are you sure that's the army you heard the guards talking about?'

'I'm not one hundred per cent sure, it's more of a gut feeling. I just know that *this* army was needed here within the city walls.'

'That means Crawford Reign knows about them,' I said softly, piecing together the macabre facts. Was it possible that he was behind the murders of his own people?

'Yes, I believe he does. The captain of the guard was ordering his men to clean the riders' uniforms and return them to the basement.'

'Basement? Isn't that where you thought Cassias the sorcerer was?'

Theo nodded. 'It's looking more likely that Cassias is alive and still within the city and probably using the Black Riders to do his bidding.'

'So the lord might *not* know about it?' I didn't know why I sounded so hopeful. Crawford Reign gave me the creeps. Being in his presence was the most uncomfortable I'd felt in years, but somewhere deep within me, I wanted to believe that despite being a manipulative worm he was loyal to the city and faithful to his people.

'I'm just speculating,' Theo said, dropping down onto the spare bed. 'Those girls were destined for somewhere within the city, and I do believe that Cassias is involved even if Crawford isn't.'

There was a long silence as each of us contemplated the information we'd just heard. I didn't want to believe that the city was so corrupt and dangerous. Theo's father was a classic example of the good that existed. But Theo's father wasn't here. The lord had sent him away too. My stomach flipped at the implications. Was Theo in danger or would he be protected against whatever was rising?

'We need to get out of the city,' I said, breaking the silence.

'Agreed,' Robbie said, nudging Newt awake.

Theo looked at each of us in turn, his jaw set in a hard line.

'There's only one way I can think of to get you safely out of the city, but you're not going to like it.'

Theo wasn't kidding when he said we wouldn't like our escape route. The bodies of the dead pressed up against me, and I fought the gag reflex as Theo carefully laid another corpse over me.

Robbie hadn't batted an eye when Theo explained his idea, and even Newt had only recoiled for a second. I, on the other hand, had a full-on freak-out.

The wagon was large with wooden slats around three sides to prevent bodies from toppling off as it moved through the streets. Theo had attached the horses before getting us into position and recommended that Newt lay in between Robbie and me near the back of the wagon, closer to the driver's seat. There were ten dead bodies in total, all wrapped in cream silk and brown cord.

The smell was intense, and I pressed my hand against my nose and mouth a little harder. If we survived this escape, I was fairly sure I'd never have a good night's sleep ever again.

'Ready?' I heard Theo hiss from somewhere to my left.

'Yeah!' Robbie answered from my right, his voice muffled by the mound of flesh above him. I gagged again.

The wagon jolted, and I whimpered. Newt kicked me in the leg, and I tried to calm my racing heart. He was right; if I didn't pull myself together before we reached the guard on duty then we'd be caught and thrown in the prison cells, or worse.

I had no idea how far the small church was from the back gate. Theo had explained the burial procedure to us before we left. Bodies were kept in the vault beneath the church, and once a week Theo and his father would anoint them, wrap the bodies, and transport them to the burial site. In essence, the burial site was just a large hole in the ground on the outskirts of the city within a sacred space. There was a back gate leading to a narrow footpath where the holy man had to carry each body across the tar moat and then navigate a wooden bridge suspended over the rocks to a graveyard.

'*No wonder your dad always looks so fit and healthy,*' Robbie had said. '*His arm muscles would put Xander's to shame!*'

Once we made it through the guards and out through the gate, we would have to wait until Theo had carried all the bodies to the graveyard before sliding down from the cart and following him across the narrow path and bridge. We would be fully exposed should any of the guards choose to monitor that section of the back gate, but it was the only way of making it out of the city and avoiding the guards who were rushing through the streets searching for their escaped prisoner.

It was then a long trek from the graveyard around the perimeter of the city and out to the plains but taking our time was preferable to being captured.

'Halt!'

The wagon came to a stop and jolted slightly as Theo climbed down from the driver's seat. I strained to listen through the many layers of bone and flesh.

'What you got there?'

'I'm transporting the dead to the graveyard,' Theo said. His voice was a little higher than usual. My stomach churned. He needed to act normal, or they would suspect something wasn't right.

'It's a bit late for that, isn't it?'

We'd prepared for this. The holy man tended to take the burial cart out at dusk to avoid the hottest part of the day, but with him away on his pilgrimage Theo could pull the *I have to cope all on my own* card.

'I'm a bit behind with my chores if I'm honest,' Theo said. 'With my father away I'm struggling to get it all done.'

There was a long wait, and I started to think the guard hadn't bought it, but then he shouted Theo forward. We were out.

The wagon trundled forward until it passed through the back gate and Robbie and Newt lying beside me gave audible sighs of relief. Only a few more feet and we'd be able to shed our morbid cloak and get my brother to safety.

'Stop!'

I froze at the sound of a new voice. An authoritative voice. The sound of several pairs of boots scraped the ground around the wagon.

'Bit late for burying the dead, isn't it, son?'

Theo cleared his throat. 'As I've already explained, I'm behind on my chores since my father left for his pilgrimage. We normally do this together.'

I held my breath as I waited to see if the new arrival would believe Theo's story. I didn't have to wait long.

'We've had a dangerous prisoner escape from the cells this evening, and the city is on high alert.'

'Oh my goodness, I had no idea, Captain. I'm so sorry. If I'd been aware of the problem, I would never have left the church.'

Silence.

'That's okay. It's in hand. We have the entire guard out looking for him.'

'He must be a dangerous prisoner indeed if he warrants the entire guard. Is he a murderer?'

A shuffle of boots and a small cough.

'No, nothing so macabre, but he is of special interest to our lord so I'm sure you can understand the urgency.'

I flinched. Robbie would want to know why Newt was of special interest to Crawford Reign and I'd be forced to explain his ultimatum.

'Of course, Captain. I'll get my chores done as quickly as possible and then be back at the church before you know it.'

Theo tapped the side of the wagon as if reassuring the dead that their journey was about to continue.

'Nonsense, I'll have my guards help you with the burial. As I said, the prisoner is dangerous, and the lord would never forgive me if anything happened to his holy man's son.'

Damn it.

I squeezed my free hand around the handle of my dagger as the wagon began to move once more. How many guards had he assigned to Theo? Could we take them all?

We eventually came to a rocking halt, and the back of the cart dropped open and clattered against the floor. The wrapped bodies began to move; one by one they were dragged from the cart and taken to the graveyard. We had a small reprieve between each round trip as the guards could only carry one body at a time.

'You need to move as soon as the next bodies are taken away,' Theo whispered from somewhere near my ear. 'Do you understand?'

Robbie knocked against the wooden floor, and Theo humphed to acknowledge that his warning had been heeded.

'Thank you so much, gentlemen, I don't know what I would have done without you,' Theo said too loudly. 'If you could take these three next that would be great.'

Three. That meant there must be three guards. Could we take them out between us? I couldn't reach my bow and arrows as they were trapped beneath my body, but I did have access to my blade, and I knew Robbie had his sword in hand too.

The thought of taking another life made me nauseous, but if it came to a choice between them and us I knew I wouldn't hesitate. Robbie was right; killing did change you.

The crushing weight of the dead lifted as the guards removed another body from the cart. I could see the stars above and feel the wisps of cool night air. We were still obscured from view by the last couple of cadavers but as soon as the guards returned they would discover us.

I could see Theo standing at the back of the cart waving his hands around as he directed the guards. His skin was covered in a sheen of sweat, but I didn't think it was from any physical exertion. He was barely holding it together.

His eyes flickered in our direction, and he caught me watching him. With a short nod, he jumped off the wagon and moved out of my line of sight.

'No, no, you need to lay them this way round.' His voice got quieter as he walked further away and I realised he was causing a distraction.

'Move!' I hissed, giving Newt a hard shove.

As one we uncurled from beneath the white sheets and shuffled to the edge of the wagon. In the distance, Theo was rearranging the dead and trying to engage the guards in helping. They were all facing the small mausoleum at the far end of the graveyard, which meant they had their backs to us.

Our only escape was across the path and then the narrow bridge or swimming through the tar pit and descending into the moat to take our chances with the choking vines and jagged rocks. Looking at Newt's exhausted face, I knew the latter route was a no-go. Robbie edged forward quickly, and Newt fell into step behind him. They looked like they'd done this sort of thing before and I had to block that off into a small compartment in my mind. I pulled my hood up tight over my head and followed. We took small crouched steps along the path and manoeuvred the wooden bridge with slow, calm movements, inching closer and closer to the guards and Theo, but also closer to freedom. If Theo could keep them occupied, there was no reason for them to turn around and spot us.

Robbie reached the graveyard first and stood watch as Newt and I came up behind him. The bodies were in two neat rows, and Theo stood with his hands on his hips assessing their work and praising the guards on a job well done. He was playing his part so well, and I made a mental note to thank him from the bottom of my heart if I ever saw him again.

'Stop where you are!'

I nearly jumped out of my skin as two guards came scurrying across the bridge behind us. Theo's guards whirled around at the sound and drew their swords.

My bow was in my hand and drawn within seconds. I pointed the arrow at Theo's heart.

'Stop, or I'll shoot the holy man's son,' I shouted, loud enough for them all to hear.

The colour drained from Theo's face, and his eyes darted from guard to guard as if waiting for one of them to step up and save him. From beneath my hood I watched every emotion roll over my friend's face.

'What are you doing?' Robbie hissed.

His expression was one of shock and horror as I nudged him and Newt behind me. Did he honestly believe I would shoot my friend?

I backed away, pushing them further away from the guards. My heart was threatening to burst out of my chest, but the arrow remained steady. Beneath my skin tiny vibrations stirred again and I saw the flickers of white light ignite at my fingertips. I shook it off. Now wasn't the time to marvel at my mage magic.

'Nobody moves or I shoot.'

The guards on the bridge had paused, but those surrounding Theo were beginning to inch forward.

'We're at the border.' Robbie spoke softly over my shoulder instructing me that we'd reached the way out.

'Get Newt out of here,' I breathed back at him. 'I'll be right behind you.'

The boys ran for the border where the graveyard met the edge of the wilderness. Beyond this, there was nothing but forest and fields, which eventually bled into the parched landscape of the plains. It had been Theo's suggestion to get Newt to the plains, and I prayed that Robbie would follow through on that if anything happened to me.

'You won't get away with this, boy,' spat the guard closest to Theo.

I smiled beneath my hood. Perfect. Let them think I was a boy, let them send the entire guard out for a hooded boy with a bow, and let it drive them mad when they never found him.

I raised my arm and pulled back on the bowstring. The guards froze, and I used this to my advantage. Letting the arrow fly in Theo's direction, I used their panicked reaction to run off into the darkness, and as I hurried away, I prayed that I'd missed.

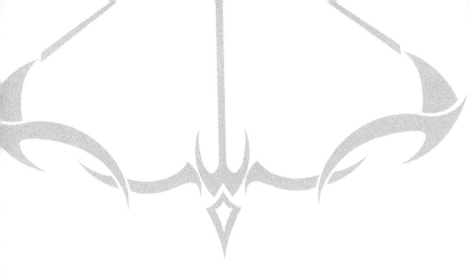

SEVEN

My brother was grinning when I eventually caught up with them in a copse of trees. His face was filthy, his clothes torn, and he looked feral, but also the happiest I'd seen him in a long while.

'That was amazing!'

He threw himself into my arms as I placed my bow on the ground at their feet. My hands were shaking, and the pounding in my head was beyond anything I'd experienced before.

'What was?' I feigned innocence but knew he was referring to me threatening my friend.

'Those stupid guards didn't know what to do.' He laughed again. 'They just stood there like idiots.'

I smiled at his exuberance and hugged him tight, but over the top of his head, I met Robbie's gaze.

'Is Theo okay?'

I took a deep breath to settle the giant bats that had once again invaded my insides and shrugged my shoulders. 'I hope so.'

Newt took a step back and looked up at me, his wide, expressive eyes shining with an odd look I'd never seen before. 'Did you shoot your friend?'

I shrugged again. 'I fired the arrow in his direction, but I don't think it struck him.'

'Whoa, that's not good, Maz. He helped us to escape. You really shouldn't shoot your friends.'

I couldn't help the nervous giggle that escaped as I ruffled his hair.

'I didn't plan on shooting my friend, Newt, and I certainly *tried* to avoid hurting him, but I had to give the guards something to panic over so I could escape.'

Robbie turned away.

'What?' I shouted at his back. 'Would you have done anything differently?'

'No, I wouldn't,' he said quietly, 'but I'm just some nobody who lives on the plains, hunts the lord's meat, steals, and lies. I thought you were better than that.'

It felt like a slap in the face and stung just as much. I blinked away the tears that welled up.

'We need to get out of here before they send the entire guard out looking for us,' Robbie added before moving off into the darkness.

Newt and Robbie strode off ahead, and I dragged my feet behind them. Theo would be okay. I wasn't one hundred per cent sure of that fact, but I had to hope that my scare tactics had been just that and nothing more serious.

I flexed my fingers and searched for the earlier sensations I'd felt. Every time I experienced intense emotions the crackling and bubbling would begin within me. Was this the magic that Mage Hall had spoken about? I kicked myself for not finding out more before I dismissed him as crazy.

I'd only recently used my bow to kill a man, I didn't think I was physically or emotionally prepared to master the art of defence using mage magic as well. Not when I had so much to think about.

Back in Theo's comfortable city home we'd talked about getting Newt to the plains and how keeping a low profile was imperative, but Theo had also suggested that I needed to stay in the Link if I wanted Crawford Reign to believe I had nothing to do with my brother's escape.

Maybe it was the right thing to do. I could leave Newt in Robbie's care and return to the Link. I'd never wanted to leave our home in the first place, but the stupid blessing ceremony and Crawford's unwanted attention had come along and changed everything for us.

Xander and Fergus would be worried sick when we didn't materialise from the moat as planned, but they would also have their hands full with the three girls we'd rescued.

There was something evil going on in the city and if I stayed in the Link perhaps I could help Theo uncover the details and set it right. That's if Theo ever spoke to me again.

'What are you thinking about?' Newt hung back until I caught him up and slipped his hand into mine.

'I was just thinking about how I need to get back to the Link before anyone notices I'm gone.'

Robbie came to a sudden stop in front of us.

'Are you insane?' he said. 'Why would you go back to the Link?'

'The guards back at the churchyard called me *boy*, they don't know it was me who helped Newt escape, and if I go home, I can feign ignorance and act the part of the distraught sister. I petitioned the lord for Newt's release and it would be a clear sign of guilt if I vanished from our home the same night my brother escaped. Besides, it was Theo's idea.'

Storm clouds billowed in Robbie's eyes as he studied me. We'd worked well together tonight, made a good team, but we lived very different lives, and even though I needed him to keep my brother safe I knew my destiny followed an alternative path.

'What if the guards put two and two together? What then? You and Theo will be thrown in a cell and left to rot. That's if the holy man's son ever speaks to you again.'

Ouch. I'd apparently hit a nerve with my actions, but I couldn't dwell on that right now.

'All I ask is that you keep Newt safe and leave the rest up to me. The girls we rescued tonight were part of something bigger, and I need to be close to the city if we stand any chance of finding out what's going on.'

'So you're planning on taking Crawford and the Black Riders on single-handed then?' There was an air of amusement in his tone.

'No, I don't intend on going anywhere near Crawford Reign, but you've seen what's going on in the lower towns. People are dying out on the plains, and somehow the Black Riders, the lord, and Cassias are involved. I want to help our people. I want to help my brother live a free life. I want...'

Robbie stepped forward and took my face in his hands.

'And I want you to stay alive.'

I was stunned into silence. Newt coughed in the background and broke the spell. Robbie's hands dropped from my face, and he stormed off into the trees calling for my brother to follow.

Newt hung back briefly to hug me.

'Stay safe, Maz. Don't do anything stupid...again.'

I laughed and kissed the top of his head.

'Look after Robbie, Xander, and Fergus, won't you. Those boys will get into trouble if you don't keep an eye on them.'

He puffed his little chest out and grinned up at me.

'I will,' he said.

Newt darted off into the darkness after Robbie, and I sucked in a deep breath. I hoped that my plan wasn't a foolish one and that I could succeed. I pondered this as I wound my way through the deserted streets to my home, hiding my bow and arrow beneath a fallen tree just outside the village. If the guards decided to search our hut, they wouldn't find any weapon to show that I'd played a part in Newt's escape.

Crawford Reign wasn't an idiot even if he was a creep and it would require all my strength to play the part I needed to, but by pretending to be the anxious sister I could stay in the Link and find out more information to help our people; then it would be worth it.

The pile of blankets was still in the middle of the floor when I arrived home. I tidied up and changed into a plain woollen dress, stashing my hooded cloak under the pig trough behind the house. Waking up beside Robbie seemed like such a long time ago and as I sat on my cot a wave of exhaustion washed over me. I lay on my bed and drifted off into a deep and troubled sleep.

The loud commotion in the street outside pulled me from my slumber, and I opened my eyes to the bright sunshine streaming through the windows. My head felt foggy and as I poured a jug of water into my washbowl the previous night's events steamrolled through my mind.

I had to hope that Newt and Robbie had made it safely to the plains and been reunited with Xander and Fergus. Maybe I should have insisted on them getting a message to me.

As I pondered on the whereabouts of my friends I was interrupted by shouts and cheers. Whatever was going on out there held an air of excitement and trepidation although the low-level grumbles of the folk from the lower town eclipsed some of the merriment. Curiosity got the better of me, and I pulled back the curtain to get a better view of the street.

My heart crashed to a halt in my chest as I watched twenty of the lord's guard making their way through the winding tracks toward me. They held their banners aloft, which signalled that the Lord of Obanac and his entourage were in convoy. I dug my fingernails into the wooden door frame as the black hood of the lord's carriage came into view, the gold trim shimmering in the sunlight.

No! It wasn't possible. The lord was heading this way. Crawford Reign, surrounded by his elite guard, was in the Link, among his people, and heading straight for my home.

'Isn't it wonderful, Maz?' shouted my neighbour. 'At last the young lord is taking an interest in our community.'

I smiled and waved a trembling hand in the air as if to mirror her celebration, but in truth, I was struggling not to be violently sick.

The procession came to a standstill as they reached my row of huts, the carriage seemingly too big to fit down the narrow run of homes. I could see Crawford's black hair above the crowds that had gathered.

Why was he here? He must know about Newt's escape by now, but surely he would have sent his guards to question me, not do it himself, in person. Was this another ploy to get me to give in to his demands? Whatever it was I had to stay strong.

My vision began to blur, and my mouth became dry as he approached. I had to remember the plan. Act surprised. Act shocked. Play the innocent and distraught sister.

The closer he got, the more I believed I was going to be caught out. Robbie was right; I should never have done this. When they left for the plains, I should have gone with them. Survive and thrive, that's what my motto should be, not stay and die.

'Marianne!' Crawford Reign stood before me in a lavish black cloak with jewelled edging and large billowing sleeves. Although I couldn't deny that he was striking to look at, his dark eyes told me everything I needed to know.

'My lord.' I curtseyed but kept my gaze on his. 'What a surprise. Have you come to discuss the terms of my brother's release?'

It was a bold move on my part to question the unanswered correspondence I'd sent him over the last few days, and I didn't miss the flicker of contempt behind those black eyes. Had he come out to the Link to see for himself if I was here?

I moved aside to allow him access to my home. Now wasn't the time to think about the unmade bed or the pile of Newt's clothes that permanently lived in the corner unless we had company. It was time to stay calm and focus on our plan. Time to act the part I'd given myself in this story.

'Please, sit down.' I set a chair in the centre of the room for the lord, but he chose to ignore it and explore his surroundings instead.

'You have a lovely home, Marianne,' he said. 'I see why you weren't eager to leave it behind and join me in the city.'

I was speechless. Had he accepted that he wasn't going to win this time?

It was difficult to know what to make of the situation. Crawford Reign was in my house, lifting my books to read the titles, admiring a quilt that my mother had made when I was a little girl, and smelling the small posy of flowers that sat on the table. He had entered alone, leaving his guards outside to deal with the evergrowing and inquisitive crowd.

'Your brother escaped from the cells last night.' He stopped moving about and stood motionless in the centre of the floor, his eyes drilling into mine.

Heat rushed up my face and tears welled in the corner of my eyes. *Act surprised. Act shocked.*

'I...I don't understand, how could this happen? He's just a boy.' I let the tears fall and hunched my shoulders as I circled my arms around myself. 'He's just a boy,' I repeated.

The lord didn't move for a moment as he watched me sob and splutter.

'He was aided by two men who murdered my guards and stole a precious cargo. Do you have any idea who they could be, Marianne?'

I wiped at the tears on my face as I tried to stop the shaking. I didn't know if I was still acting or if I'd gone into shock from the severity of my situation. Precious cargo? Did he mean the girls—the sacrifice? I tried to push the thought of him butchering young girls with his wicked sorcerer to one side as I played my part.

'We don't have any men in our lives, my lord. Our father was sent away by your father many years ago. We only have each other. Nobody would have any interest in my brother.'

Crawford winced at the mention of his father.

'I'm so sorry, my lord, I didn't mean to upset you by mentioning your father.'

He turned away from me, but I wasn't sure if it was sadness or anger that clouded his expression. I pushed a little further.

'It's hard being left to cope on your own, isn't it? I know our situations are vastly different but I do understand what it feels like. I only have to be responsible for one small boy whereas you have the entire kingdom to care for.'

He whirled around in a blaze of black fabric and loathing. His eyes burned with a hatred I'd never seen before.

'My father left me with a broken kingdom and rotting corpses littering the land. He didn't care what happened to his people; he was too wrapped up in grief to care about anyone.'

The brutality of his words astonished me. Was I seeing the boy behind the man's mask? A boy who lost his mother and was then abandoned by a grieving father? I sucked in a deep breath and stepped forward placing my hand on his arm.

He flinched but didn't move away; instead, he studied my hand resting on his arm as if it were some new and interesting invention worthy of exploration.

'Thank you for your counsel, Marianne.' He laughed without humour. 'Perhaps I should enlist you as an advisor at the castle and get rid of the stuffy old men who insist on telling me what to do?'

Theo suspected that Crawford Reign was connected to the evil that plagued the city, but was it possible that he was just another innocent within the sea of corruption? A wave of compassion washed over me and without thinking I took the lord's hands in mine.

'You have the power to unite all of your people and bring happiness to the realm, my lord.'

Time stood still inside my tiny hut. The morning sunshine caught the dust mites floating in the air as they danced around our motionless bodies. In the background the endless chatter of an excitable crowd filled the space around us, and yet time had stopped. I felt like I was standing in a giant bubble of nothingness waiting for the audible pop when the bubble burst.

What on earth had possessed me to grasp his hands so tightly and be so familiar with him? I was trying to appeal to a cold-hearted and clinical city lord who had, only recently, informed me of his desire to be with me and keep me within the walls.

Let go of his hands! Let go of his hands! These were the only words I could hear screaming inside my brain and yet I clung on. I wasn't sure why.

Crawford looked as astonished as I was, but he hadn't moved away. He didn't smack my hands away or call out for his guard. It was only then I realised he was clinging on too.

It happened so fast, and before either of us could release our hands, Crawford Reign stepped close and kissed me.

It was hard and rough, his stubble scratching at my chin. I'd never been kissed before, and this was not how I'd imagined it would be. Robbie's face flashed through my mind, and a wave of nausea coursed through me at the thought of explaining this to him. I tried to pull away, but Crawford released my hands, trapping me against him. I put my palms on his chest and pushed, trying to dislodge him, but he was strong.

We stumbled backwards, my back hitting the wall of the hut and pinning me between it and him. Panic set in as he pulled at my dress, lifting the skirts to run his hand up my leg. I stomped down on his foot causing him to leap back in surprise. My mind was spinning and my lips felt swollen. I straightened my skirts, and before I could think logically, I'd lifted my arm and slapped Crawford Reign hard across the face.

'Guards!' he screamed.

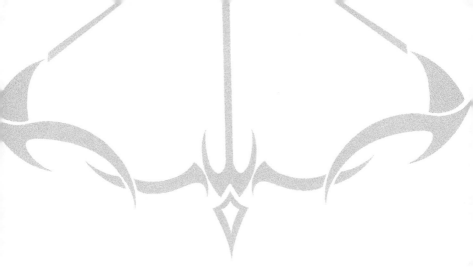

EIGHT

Everything happened in a blur following my enthusiastic retaliation to the lord's kiss. He had stormed out of my hut snapping orders at the guards as he went, the billowing black fabric of his cloak hurrying down the track and vanishing from sight.

The residents of the Link scattered as soon as they saw Crawford Reign's face. It resembled an apocalyptic world of storm clouds, tornados, and fiery dragons circling the skies. In reality, he only had a bright red cheek, but you would think from his actions that a great catastrophe had befallen him.

My world imploded when the first person through my door following Crawford's departure was his scar-faced guard, the same guard who had given Newt the apple and thrown him in a prison cell.

'You!' I cried, hitting out at him as he grabbed my arm and dragged me out into the street. 'Get your hands off me.'

Being manhandled out of my own home by the lord's elite guard was not something I ever thought I would experience, yet I felt strangely exhilarated. My neighbours watched from behind their shutters and doors, hiding their faces and their children, but I didn't care. I'd gone to them once and asked for their help, but now I understood. They were afraid of the situation I now found myself in. They feared for their lives and that of their families. This was not a safe world to live in, and as I was jostled down the track by Scarface I vowed to help the people in the Link, and the lower towns, and all the people on the plains. I made a silent promise to myself that I would save them all from the tyranny of the city.

The guard escorted me along the same route I had walked with Newt to my blessing, only this time there was no brightly coloured bunting fluttering in the breeze, or cheerful faces waving and applauding my arrival.

I was expecting to be taken to the cells, probably thrown into the same one my brother recently vacated, as a point of irony; instead, Scarface led me up the hill to the back of the castle.

'Where are you taking me?' I snapped, tugging on his arm once more just because I knew it irritated him.

'You'll find out soon enough.'

We walked some distance, passing the main castle buildings and the servants' quarters and ended up standing at the foot of a large tower. It was a building I knew well. The tower could be seen from far away, a beacon that told any traveller they would soon be arriving in the city. It had also once been a place of terror and death.

Spikes jutted out from the stone walls at the higher levels where beheaded criminals once kept a lifeless vigil over the realm. In the days before the phantom's curse swept across the land the tower had been used to house the army of the damned: fierce warriors whose sole goal was to kill. They were soulless creatures, neither man nor beast. Davis Reign had closed the tower during his time in the lord's chair, and as I stood before the dark stone, I feared that his son had resurrected it to its former glory once more.

I pulled hard on my arm until it was free of Scarface's grasp. I couldn't make a run for it or fight my way out of this one, but I wasn't about to let this man take me into the tower without an explanation.

'Why are we here?' I folded my arms across my chest in the same way I'd seen Robbie do. It gave me a slight air of *whatever* which is no doubt what Robbie hoped to achieve when he did it, but it also made me feel closer to him somehow. Mimicking his stance, the same stance that used to annoy me so much, helped me to shield myself from whatever was about to happen.

'Our Lord has requested that you reside in the tower until he needs you.' His smarmy grin distorted his face even further, stretching the scar in a grotesque manner.

'The tower hasn't been in use for years. Am I to be left here to starve to death just because I gave Crawford Reign a slap for his unwanted advances?'

Scarface chuckled. 'On the contrary, miss. The tower is quite different from the old days. You'll see what I mean.'

He didn't grab me this time; instead, he opened the lower door and gestured for me to enter. With my heart beating out of my chest, and my sweaty palms clinging to my skirts I walked inside.

The room was cool but not altogether unpleasant. There was a huge, empty fireplace opposite the door, with an assortment of pots and pans hanging from a rack above it, and a large table and benches in the centre. A set of wooden stairs hugged the interior walls of the tower. They spiralled all the way to the top creating an inner chamber. I could see to the roof high above us. All the rooms encircled this inner tower, facing out across the surrounding lands.

I'd been half expecting to find skeletons coated in cobwebs and dirty iron shackles hanging from the ceiling, but instead, I found the space to be homely, not in a crackling fire, soup in the pot, curled up in my cot kind of homely, but not disagreeable.

Scarface led me up the winding staircase to our right. The steps broke off at certain points onto small landings, each with a single wooden door. We passed four doors on the way up, each one opening up into what looked like servants' sleeping quarters. They didn't look like the sort of rooms a deadly warrior might sleep in unless the soulless army liked warm blankets and needlepoint. My mind whirled with the possibilities of what the tower was now being used for but as we reached the top my questions were answered.

The highest room in the tower was fit for a queen. Swathes of cream silk billowed from the apex to hide the grey slate roof. The fabric was fastened along the wall and cascaded down to the floor. None of the dark stone was visible beneath the cloth waterfall. A massive wooden bed covered in a rich purple velvet blanket and an assortment of gold and silver cushions dominated the room. To the left was a picture window that looked out across the realm. From this vantage point, I could see my friends and neighbours bustling about preparing for market day.

'What is this place?' The wonder in my voice made Scarface chuckle, and I returned to the present with a jolt. It might look like a fairy tale, but I was here under guard.

'It's a room fit for a lady,' he said with a hint of sarcasm.

I spun full circle taking in the dressing table with oval mirror and jewelled perfume bottles, the blanket box under the window with the initials LR carved into it, and the portrait of a young smiling couple, which hung among the folds of fabric.

The man in the picture looked strangely familiar until I realised where I'd seen him before. The eyes were different, but the handsome face and black hair gave it away. He resembled Crawford Reign, but as I studied the pretty strawberry blonde girl with shining green eyes, I knew these were, in fact, Crawford's parents, Davis and Lucy.

I glanced across at the bed once again.

'Is this where Lucy Reign died?'

Scarface laughed out loud and stomped over to the door.

'Welcome to your new home, miss.' With that, he slammed the door behind him and turned the key in the lock.

I ran after him, banging my fists against the wood and shouting obscenities at him but the sound of his boots retreating down the staircase filled the space.

No, no, no. Why would he do this? What possible purpose did Crawford have for keeping me here of all places?

I felt sick to my stomach as I looked around the room. Mrs Elrod had been a friend and confidant for Lucy Reign, but when the lord's wife died, she had been cast out of the city and banished from the security of its warding. Whatever happened in this room had caused the then lord to lose his mind and turn against his people.

Lucy Reign's death had been the catalyst which caused my own parents to be ripped from my arms and sent away to opposite ends of the realm.

Did Crawford know all of this? Was he using emotion to punish me?

I sank to the floor, pulling my knees up to my chest and hugged them close. Despite the warm and lavish surroundings a deep chill had settled in my bones. Tears began to fall as I thought about Newt, my parents, Mrs Elrod, and Robbie. Had Crawford found them? Were they all safe from harm? Was I?

I buried my face into my knees and sobbed. I cried for hours curling myself up into a ball, until eventually I started to drift off, the ghosts of the past surrounding me.

Footsteps moving around the room pulled me from my nightmares, but it took me a moment to remember where I was. The sun was high in the sky, and the grumble in my stomach confirmed that it was well past lunch.

I blinked against the brightness of the day and then saw to my horror that I was no longer alone.

A hooded man slithered across my room causing the hairs on the back of my neck to stand to attention as I watched his every movement. How did he get here? Who was he? The cloak he wore skimmed the floor and rustled like old paper when he walked. Once upon a time, I'm sure the material was rich in texture and colour, but now it was old and worn, very much in keeping with the wearer's hands, which hung from the large sleeves.

'Who are you?' My voice gave away the trepidation I felt.

The newcomer raised his hands and dropped the hood of his cloak revealing a wrinkled face and bald head. His eyes were black, like Crawford's, but unlike the lack of emotion in the lord's eyes, these had the flicker of hellfire.

I'd heard the stories around the campfires at night. I'd listened to the tales of a young soldier and his sorcerer friend who defeated the phantom's curse that kept Lady Lindley a prisoner in her own skin. I knew who it was that stood before me, but I dared not speak his name out loud. He'd vanished into the bowels of the castle before I was born and it was rumoured that he had died there. If I was right and the great sorcerer Cassias stood before me, it meant all of Theo's suspicions were correct, and the realm was in great peril.

'You are the girl Our Lord has chosen?'

I bristled at his words.

'I'm Marianne, a healer from the Link. I am *not* the girl you think I am.'

The sorcerer chuckled, but the sound held no humour.

'You are exactly who I think you are, Marianne.'

He moved closer, and I couldn't stop myself flinching away from his closeness. He wasn't affected by my reaction as he circled me sniffing the air around me and touching my red hair.

'Our Lord has chosen well. You are indeed powerful enough to withstand your role, but there's something else underneath.'

He scratched at his chin and studied me like a mage studies the herbs and moon cycles. My pulse raced under his unrelenting stare until he snapped his fingers and broke the uncomfortable spell.

'Guidance, Marianne. That's what you need. Our Lord will guide you along your rightful path.'

'What path?' Panic rose in my chest as I wondered what this evil man was referring to.

His smile looked more like a grimace as he grabbed my chin in his withered hands and pulled me close to him. His breath was rotten, and I tried to pull away, but for such an old and feeble-looking man he was strong.

'You're Cassias,' I said, unable to hold the terror in much longer.

He inclined his head as if we were being formally introduced.

'We thought you were dead or gone.'

He released my face, and I stumbled back a few paces eager to get away from the smell of death.

'Not dead, not gone, just waiting.'

'Waiting for what?'

'Waiting for you, Marianne.'

I was stunned. Why would the lord's sorcerer be waiting for me?

'You are the answer to our prayers, Marianne, and you will be more powerful than you could ever imagine.'

I was almost certain that this man had never prayed in his lifetime, and I was also sure that the power he spoke of was not something I wanted to experience.

A light tapping pulled at the corner of my mind, and it took me a few moments to realise it was coming from the door. I spun away from the sorcerer.

'Hello? Is someone there?' Hope flared in my chest.

'Are you okay, miss?' a small voice said from beyond the barrier.

'Who are you?'

'My name's Lauren, miss. I'm here to look after you. Is there anything I can get for you?'

I shook my head as if trying to dislodge the strange predicament I found myself in and the thoughts that whirled inside. Had Crawford Reign assigned me a handmaid?

Before I could answer the girl, a scratching sound behind me drew my attention, and I whirled in time to see a large swirling mass of grey and red open up in the centre of the room. Cassias gave a small bow before stepping through into the churning colour and disappearing from view. The portal closed behind him leaving me standing open-mouthed.

'Miss, are you still there?'

'I'd like to speak with the holy man's son if I may. I...I need some counsel.'

'Of course, miss. Master Theodore knows you're here and has been expecting you to ask for him. I'll send for him at once.'

Relief washed over me.

'Thank you.' I heard her move away and head down the stairs then a thought struck me. 'Lauren!'

Small footsteps came running back upstairs.

'Yes, miss.'

'I'm a bit hungry!'

Giggles.

'Okay, I'll bring you some lunch.'

My pulse quickened at the thought of seeing my friend. I was thankful that he was still looking out for me. I'd been worried that he'd never come to my aid again. Why would he? The last time I'd seen him I'd threatened his life to escape with my own. I hoped he would see that for what it was and not hold it against me. Only time would tell. I sat back on the floor and waited.

The sound of several pairs of boots outside my door raised the tiny hairs on my arms, and I worried that Scarface had returned for me before I'd had a chance to see Theo. The key turned in the lock and the door swung open. Relief rushed through me upon seeing Theo's flushed face.

He was standing behind the guards and gave me a frown and the slightest shake of his head as they all entered the room. Scarface and another, younger guard strode in, Lauren bringing up the rear with a tray of bread, meat, and cheese.

'Put it on the bed and leave,' barked Scarface.

Lauren almost dropped the tray as she stepped closer to me. I placed my hand on her trembling arm and smiled down at her.

'Thank you, Lauren.'

She grinned at me before darting out of the room and hurtling down the stairs. The food looked so good, and my stomach growled again.

'Make it last cos that's all yer getting,' Scarface growled at me.

He then followed Lauren down the stairs. Theo was still standing in the doorway, and as Scarface brushed past him, I noticed he was holding a stick.

'Are you okay?'

The younger guard placed his hand on the hilt of his sword and marched into the centre of the room. He couldn't have been more than a year older than Theo and me.

'Our holy son was wounded in battle recently,' said the guard. 'A deadly criminal escaped the city and attempted to murder him. He's lucky to be alive.'

Heat rushed up my face and a wave of nausea crashed in the pit of my stomach. I was the deadly criminal the guard spoke of.

'Oh my goodness, I hope you caught the person responsible.'

'Not yet, but he won't get far. We've got *special* guards out looking for him.'

'Special guards?' I raised an eyebrow and glanced across at Theo, who was studying a beetle on the floor as if he'd never seen one before.

'Nothing for you to worry about, miss. The boy will be caught and hanged soon enough.'

I swallowed down the bile in my throat and hoped the young soldier didn't notice my flushed cheeks as I tripped over my words. 'Oh, yes, well...that's good to hear.'

Theo limped across the threshold and held the door to steady himself.

'Soldier, I wonder if I could ask you to wait downstairs at the main door for me. I'm sure Miss Fitz doesn't need an audience for her confession.'

I smiled and dutifully nodded my head as if to confirm his words.

The guard looked from Theo to me and back again.

'My orders were to stay with you.'

'And you will be with me, soldier, but not in the same room. Giving counsel is a sacred act, and every living being deserves sanctuary and privacy for this.'

The young guard appeared to mull over Theo's words for a while until he was seemingly satisfied that I offered no threat to his charge.

'Very well, sir, I'll be downstairs if you need me.'

He stomped out of the room and closed the door behind him. I didn't hear the key turn in the lock this time, and it filled my heart with joy.

'Theo, I'm so sorry. Are you okay?'

I rushed to my friend's side and helped him limp across to the bed. He winced as he dropped down onto the soft surface.

'You shot me!' he hissed.

I sat beside him and slipped my hand into his.

'I tried not to hit anything major.'

He gawked at me for the longest moment and then his face softened and he started to laugh. He laughed so hard tears trailed down his face. I couldn't help myself as my shoulders started to shake and the bubbling laughter escaped from deep within me too.

We fell back onto the bed gasping for breath and hiccupping as the hilarity tempered the seriousness of our situation.

'I truly am sorry, Theo.'

He leaned over and kissed me gently on the cheek.

'I know. It was a bit of a shock at the time, but it's only a flesh wound, and later, when I was bandaged up and back in my bed, I understood why you did it. If we're going to beat Crawford, we need to be smarter than him, and it's so important that neither of us gets caught.'

I laughed again, sitting up and swinging my arms in a wide arc. 'It might not look like it, but this is, in fact, my prison cell.'

'I might be able to do something about that,' he said with a feral grin, 'but first, you need to tell me exactly what happened after you escaped.'

I recounted our trek through the darkness and how angry Robbie had been at me for shooting Theo and then returning to the Link instead of going to the plains with him and Newt. Theo nodded at all the appropriate moments and seemed touched that Robbie had worried about him. He offered the occasional 'hmm' and 'okay, okay' where necessary, but he didn't interrupt me as I spewed out all my thoughts and worries about the situation I was in and how anxious I was about my brother.

When I'd finished, I felt physically drained. Saying it all out loud made it real and I was all of a sudden overcome with tiredness.

'I heard you'd been brought here and knew you'd want to speak to me, so I asked Lauren to fetch me when you requested it. I also asked Lauren to send word to Robbie. He needs to know that you're okay as I'm sure news has travelled about the disturbance in the Link. I told her not to mention your opulent surroundings, or he might just think you want to be left here.'

I chuckled as I realised Robbie's ridiculous Lady of the Link title suited the current situation. If he could see me now, I'd never live it down.

'There's something else. Cassias is alive and kicking.'

'How do you know?'

'He visited me earlier and told me I was the answer to his prayers.'

Theo gulped. 'What do you think he means?'

'I have no idea,' I said. 'But let's deal with one problem at a time, shall we?'

I hoped we would find a plan for dealing with Cassias as well as my current situation.

'How am I going to get out of this, Theo? I can't even begin to understand why Crawford has put me in here.'

Theo sucked in a deep breath and struggled to his feet. He began limping back and forth across the room.

'There's something you should be aware of, Maz.'

His furrowed brow and agitated state worried me, but I waited patiently for him to continue.

'Crawford pulled all his advisors together last night. I had to stand in for my father, so I got to hear his plans. He wants to reward the people for their loyalty by installing a female figurehead into the council to act as Lady of Obanac. The lord has found someone who he feels is perfect for the future of the city: strong-willed, beautiful, and as dedicated to the people as his mother was. He told us he's chosen a girl from the Link to fill this role.'

I gasped. 'He's talking about me,' I whispered, afraid that if I spoke any louder, I might come apart at the seams. 'He intends to keep me in Obanac as a prisoner.'

'I'm afraid so. You've made quite an impression on our lord and I think the feisty slap to the face sealed the deal where he's concerned. I must say, I was surprised when he announced that you'd kissed him.'

It was my turn to pace the floor now. I wrung my hands over and over as if trying to wipe away some icky substance. Why was this happening to me?

'*He* kissed *me*,' I wailed. 'I didn't reciprocate in any way. There is no way on this earth that I would willingly kiss that man, Theo. No way! He can't believe that I would consent to this, not after everything I've said and done.'

'I don't think he's giving you much of a choice, Maz. He said that having a female confidant from the lower towns to stand with him will show the people of Obanac what a compassionate and dedicated leader he is.'

'Is he kidding? How can I act as his friend when I despise the man? Surely the people would see through him, see through us!'

Theo stiffened next to me.

'Of course!' he yelled. 'It's starting to make sense. I've listened to the murmurs from the council and they believe that someone is manipulating Crawford.'

The colour drained from my face as I understood what Theo meant.

'Cassias!'

The panic attack was swift as it rose up from my gut and tightened my chest like a vice. I clawed at my throat trying to grapple for air. Theo was by my side as I slid to the floor, catching me and cradling my trembling body in his arms. His soothing voice calmed my nerves, and my breathing soon returned to normal.

'Cassias told me that Crawford would guide me along my rightful path and make me powerful. They're working together, Theo.'

'We've got to get you out of here,' he said.

'I hope you've got a plan.'

Theo smiled at me, stroking my hair. 'I do, but when you get out of the city I need you to find Robbie and Newt in the mountains. If they did as I asked they should have found my friend Halia by now. She'll be able to offer you help and shelter and she'll have the answers we seek. Promise me you'll go to her.'

I nodded as I nestled my head against his chest.

'I promise,' I said. 'Now, what's your plan to get me out of here?'

NINE

Hurting my friend again was not something I ever planned on doing and yet here we were about to pull off a violent scam involving the holy man's son and a member of the elite guard.

'All set?' Theo asked as he readied himself.

'Are you sure I can't just jump out of the window instead?'

'It's a seven-story building, Maz. You'll either die from the fall or break every bone in your body and then die from your internal injuries.'

'I'm not comfortable with this,' I said, clutching the wooden leg Theo had broken off the elaborate chair in the corner of the room.

'Oh, but you were okay shooting an arrow in me?'

I rolled my eyes and he chuckled.

'Look, we have to make it appear realistic otherwise Crawford will think I've helped you. As soon as he knows you've escaped I'll be questioned and if I've got a bloody head, a mild concussion, and a plausible story for how I didn't see which direction you ran in, we've got a chance of pulling it off.'

'Fine, but if the city healers can't fix you up don't moan at me.'

He nodded at me and I sucked in a lungful of air. Knocking my friend out with a chair leg wasn't going to be easy.

Theo reached over and opened the door listening for the soldier he'd sent downstairs.

'He's still there,' Theo mouthed at me. 'As soon as you knock me out I want you to scream as loud as you can and he'll come running.'

I nodded and gripped the wooden leg tighter. 'What if he overpowers me?' I whispered.

'He won't. He'll be too interested in my body on the floor and won't expect you to jump out at him from behind the door.'

I took another deep breath in to steady my nerves. If Theo's plan worked, in the next few minutes I would be free.

'Ready?'

'Ready!'

I swung the leg as hard as I could and felt the sickening thud as it struck Theo on the side of the head. He dropped to the floor with a thump and I quickly checked that he was still breathing. Blood spread across the wooden floor from the wound and my stomach roiled.

I needed to act fast. Theo had no idea if Scarface was going to come back and check on us and if that happened our plan would be for nothing. One guard I could handle but not Crawford's henchman.

I opened my mouth and screamed.

The sound of the soldier clattering up the stairs echoed around the tower and I slid behind the door to wait.

It didn't take him long to reach the top floor and burst into the room. Theo was right. The soldier's first action was to check on my friend, and as he leaned over I crept out from my hiding place and swung the chair leg a second time.

The soldier slumped forward landing side by side with Theo, their blood mingling together.

'Please be okay,' I whispered to them both before bolting out of the door.

I flew down the stairs as quickly and quietly as I could even though my heart was pounding so loud the entire realm could have heard it.

The front door of the tower was ajar and I braced myself for the possibility that another guard might be outside. It was clear.

I wanted to breathe a sigh of relief but I wasn't free yet. Theo had told me about a hidden door in the city walls, one of the many dotted throughout Obanac, and my task was to find that door without being spotted and then make my way to the mountains.

I rounded the corner and sprinted for the walls. A lone figure stepped out from behind an animal pen and I slapped my hands over my mouth to stop from crying out.

Lauren grinned at me and pointed behind her at the twisting branches of ivy that coated one section of the wall.

'The door's behind the shrubs, miss,' she said. 'Take care of yourself.'

I squeezed her hand as I ran past, grateful that there were some people in this realm who still believed in good over evil.

Fergus and Xander were waiting for me at Ely's village as I made my way through the plains to the mountains, and their cries of joy upon seeing me filled me with happiness. I hadn't seen the boys since our escape from the city the night we rescued Newt and it was hard to comprehend how much had happened since then.

'It's about time you showed up!' Fergus said with a laugh.

'Did you miss me?'

'We've all missed you, Maz,' said Xander as he scooped me up into a tight hug.

I giggled at my friend's exuberance before glancing around the village.

'They're not here,' said Fergus. 'Robbie took your brother into the mountains so he'd be safe.'

My heart skipped a beat at the thought of Robbie doing the right thing. Part of me had wondered if he'd leave Newt behind and continue on his own campaign, but from the warm smiles I was getting from Fergus and Xander it appeared he'd taken caring for my brother seriously.

'We received a message from a young lass that you were on your way so Robbie asked us to wait here to meet you.'

'We're to take you to them,' Xander added. 'I think the little one is eager to see his sister.'

The thought of seeing Newt again had spurred me on through the daring escape from the tower and the journey over the plains, and I couldn't wait to be reunited with him.

I gestured for the boys to lead the way. 'Let's go then.'

The smoke curled around our feet lifting to envelop our shins and knees.

'It's there!' Xander thrust his meaty finger out in front of us highlighting the passage through to Halia's hidden cave.

'We probably should have warned you about Theo's creepy friend,' said Fergus.

'She's not creepy, she lives in a creepy cave, that's all.'

I couldn't help the smile that tugged at my lips watching these two muscular boys tiptoeing through the trees.

'Okay, so maybe Halia's not that creepy, but the scary smoke and the rustling leaves give me the chills.'

'That's what keeps the caves safe,' Xander said, pushing aside the branches of a tree so I could pass.

Up ahead was a slim opening carved out of the mountainside. Ivy clung to the rock like a leafy curtain. It would have obscured the mouth of the cave had the smoke tendrils not pulled them aside like ghostly fingers.

'I don't think I'll ever get used to this,' said Fergus with a roll of his dark eyes.

'You can always stay out here and keep guard,' Xander said, brushing past him.

'Oh yeah, so I can get eaten by a dragon. Not a chance.'

Fergus pushed ahead of us until he was level with the greenery.

The blackness of the narrow passageway was total. We clung to the wall as we felt our way along.

'M a r i a n n e.'

The voice carried on a light breeze to where I stood frozen to the spot, but it was as if someone had sighed into my ear.

'What was that?' I whispered, the hairs on my arms standing to attention.

'That would be Halia, Theo's creepy friend!' Fergus said, squeezing past me.

'She's not creepy,' Xander said again, tutting at his friend.

Glancing ahead, I noticed a faint twinkle of light further along the stone corridor.

'Let's go meet Halia then,' I said.

The corridor opened up into a cavernous space. A black pool occupied the centre with a ridge of rock circling its murky edge. Beyond the water stood two tall rock pillars and standing between them was the most beautiful girl I'd ever seen. Her raven hair hung in waves down her back, tumbling over her shoulders, and she wore a figure-hugging velvet gown as red as the brightest ruby.

'She's a nymph,' Fergus muttered to me before moving away to sit by Xander.

I gave a little wave of my hand in greeting and moved toward Halia but I was distracted by Newt and Robbie walking out from another opening in the cave.

'Maz!'

My brother threw himself into my arms and I clung to him, tears pooling in my eyes. I'd come so close to never seeing him again thanks to Crawford Reign, and not just because he had stolen my brother from me, but because of his plans to hold me in Obanac against my will. I couldn't dwell on that now and didn't want it to taint our reunion.

I looked up at Robbie and smiled through the tears. 'Thank you for keeping him safe.'

'Not a problem,' he said, kicking at a pebble on the floor. 'He was impatient to see you again, but Halia looked after us well while we waited.'

I suddenly remembered the nymph and untangled myself from Newt so I could officially introduce myself.

Halia smiled and stepped away from the rock pillars, descending the stone steps and approaching me with effortless grace.

'I'm Marianne,' I said. 'Theo told me you could help us.'

'I know who you are, Marianne, and I know why you're here. Theodore is a good soul and has sent many lost spirits my way over the years, but this is the first time he's sent humans.'

I frowned and took a small step back, pulling Newt behind me.

Halia giggled. 'I simply meant that I help the dead find a place in the mountain realm. The evil spirits you fear so much that wander the woods are just lost souls waiting to find peace. Theo guides their final dreams so I can do my work.'

'Well, if he trusts you then I trust you,' I said. 'I've left Theo behind in the city but he was eager that I visit you. We think that the realm may be in danger from Crawford Reign and his men.' I chose not to tell Halia and my friends that the reason I'd left Theo behind was because I'd knocked him out with a chair leg.

'I agree, and I believe that if the lord could wield any form of mage power he would try to harness it for his own desires. He is not a man to trust.'

'Ain't that the truth,' Fergus added.

'The worst possible evil is awakening,' Halia continued. 'Black magic is swelling within the city and leaking out across the realm. The wards that you think protect the people are only keeping them trapped inside. The wicked sorcerer grows in strength once again as he feeds off Crawford's rage.'

'You mean Cassias?'

She nodded and motioned for me to approach the water.

'It's better if I show you.'

As I watched, her eyes rolled back into her head and the water in the pool beside me began to ripple as a cool breeze whipped up around us. Halia raised her arms and swayed to and fro as if dancing to a beat only she could hear. The surface of the pool bubbled and hissed before clearing to show a scene of terror, fire, and blood. Crawford Reign stood in the centre of the image with a bloodied sword in his hand. Those black eyes burned with hellfire as he watched his people die. The scene shifted to show two black thrones and an undead army. Faces I knew and loved floated across the surface of the water. Mrs Elrod and my neighbours from the Link, Ely and the children on the plains, and then a face I knew better than my own. Newt drifted into view, his cheeks sunken and his face ashen. Sores and boils scarred his skin, but it was his eyes that tore a hole in my heart. They were the eyes of the dead.

Newt, Mrs Elrod, and the rest of my friends stood to the rear of Crawford Reign as he looked out over the lands that ran red with blood. A cloaked man stood to the lord's right holding a pulsating crystal. His head was as bald as that of a newborn, but the loathing and blood lust in his eyes showed none of the qualities of an innocent but every characteristic of pure evil. He was muttering something under his breath, and as I struggled to stay focused on the images, my friends' corpses became animated by some deep, dark evil that swirled overhead like a diseased flock of birds.

I stumbled backwards throwing my hands to my face as I did. No, no, no. It can't be.

'What did you see?' Robbie asked, reaching out to steady me as I processed the meaning behind the vision Halia had shared.

'They're resurrecting the phantom and creating an undead army.'

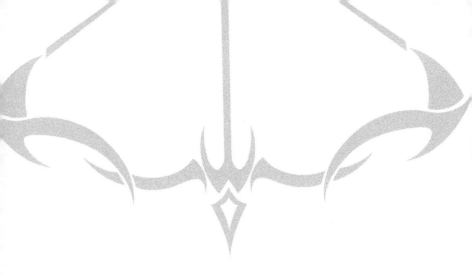

TEN

I sat some distance away from the boys as I tried to calm my rattled nerves. Being told that something terrible could unfold against witnessing it in its full multicolour glory is quite a different experience.

'I'm sorry that you had to see that, Marianne.' Halia took a seat beside me, folding the swathes of her red dress around her legs as she tucked them underneath her. She looked like a girl from the lower towns rather than a mystical nymph.

'It's okay. Theo warned me that you might show me something I wouldn't understand. I guess I wasn't expecting to see my world disappear in a flash of fire and blood before my eyes.'

'The images are only impressions of what *could* be; they're not set in stone, Marianne. The mages have whispered for many years about a new power, a pure light that would be able to bring peace to the lands. I believe that power is rising in you.'

'Me!' I looked into her warm mocha eyes and knew she was serious. 'You think I've got power over this evil?'

I waved my hand in the direction of the water which now only reflected the flicker of torchlight instead of the fire and brimstone from the earlier vision.

'That level of destruction can't be stopped by anyone, least of all me. I'm a sixteen-year-old girl from the Link. I sew, hunt, and make up healing tinctures; I don't face an evil lord, his psycho sorcerer and an undead army consisting of my loved ones.'

I took a deep breath to settle the panic that was fluttering in my gut once again. Halia chuckled and twirled a piece of her raven hair around her finger.

'I'm not asking you to stand on the battlefield alone, Marianne. I'm asking you to unite the people and show them a better way.'

'Unite the people! I tried that once when my brother was arrested. I tried to get my own friends and neighbours to join me in a bid to free him. None of them stood by me. Nobody dared to stand up to the lord then so why on earth would they do it now?'

'You must show them that you are worth fighting for. They hold hope in their hearts, Marianne, and they cling to the belief that the pure mages are right and a saviour will rise.'

'I wouldn't know where to start,' I whispered.

Halia placed her hand over my chest and leaned in close. 'Start here,' she said, tapping over my heart. 'Start believing in yourself, and soon enough others will follow.'

'I can't fight the phantom, Crawford Reign and his Black Riders, plus Cassias. It's an impossible task.'

'Nothing is impossible if you believe in yourself enough.'

'Can you help me?'

There was no denying that something magical flowed through my veins. I'd felt that sizzle and spark on a few occasions now, but if Mage Hall was right and I did possess the white mage light, I needed guidance from someone who understood its complexities and limitations.

'You already have what you need, Marianne, you just have to open yourself up to the power. You need to control it and not let the light control you.'

'O-kay, but it all sounds a bit too complicated for my liking. What if I can't control the light?'

Halia giggled. 'When you feel the magic stirring inside you, trust that you can channel it to where you need it to be.'

'So if I want to protect someone I concentrate on that person?'

'Exactly! Try it. See if you can cover me in a protective light.'

I shuffled on the spot until I sat facing Halia. She closed her eyes, which made it easier for me not to see the humour that would shine in them when I failed.

I focused on her form and tried to reach out with my mind. There was a tugging sensation from my chest as I tried to project the light to where she sat curled up like I was about to read her a bedtime story. As I reached out with the magic it snapped back, and my attention was lost.

'Relax,' Halia said, as if sensing my frustration. 'It'll come to you naturally, you don't need to force it.'

I tried again, this time painting a picture in my head of Halia surrounded in a bright white bubble. The vibration hummed through my body as thin strands of light spun from my fingertips and wrapped themselves around her body

I felt giddy as the light coated every inch of her.

'Hey Fergus, throw a pebble at me!' Halia called across to our friend, who scooped up a smooth stone and threw it in our direction.

I squealed and lost focus again, dropping the connection. The pebble bounced off Halia's shoulder and clattered to the floor by my feet.

'Oops, sorry.'

She giggled again. 'Keep practising, and you'll get the hang of it soon enough. Hopefully before Crawford Reign sends flaming boulders our way.'

I sat back with a slump, kicking the stone across the floor. A commotion near the entrance of the cave pulled me from my musings, and we both rose to see Fergus tackling a bedraggled man to the floor.

'Fergus! What are you doing?'

Robbie and Xander were at their friend's side by the time Halia and I arrived. The man sprawled out on the floor looked to be in his late forties with heavy stubble and a bloodstained tunic. He had a small cut above his eye and was struggling against Fergus, who had him pinned to the floor.

'Let him rise,' Halia said, directing a stern glare in Fergus's direction.

The man scrambled to his feet and adjusted his tunic, eyeing Fergus with contempt as he swung his attention to the nymph.

'My lady, the Black Riders returned and wiped out my village. We have nowhere else to go.'

He motioned behind him and out of the darkness men, women, and children crept forward, their faces bruised and bloody.

They kept coming, villagers from the plains helped by the folk from the lower towns, filling the cave and spilling out into the woods. Instinctively I set to work dividing everyone into groups according to their injuries.

'Xander, can you take the children who aren't wounded and make sure they have plenty of water to drink?'

'Of course,' he said, herding the older kids and carrying the smallest of the group in his arms.

'What do you need me to do?' Fergus stepped forward.

'Take the women to the side of the cave and see if any of them need a healer. If not, they can be sent outside to help the others. Send the wounded to me.'

He nodded and set off to his task.

'I want to help too.' Robbie assisted me in lifting a man onto a raised rock so that I could get a better look at his bloodied leg.

Robbie and I hadn't had much of a chance to talk since I'd arrived at the cave. I'd barely had enough time to hug Newt and explain Theo's request and the promise I'd made to him before the injured villagers began pouring into Halia's mountain home.

'I need some damp cloths to clean the wound,' I said, staring up into Robbie's blue eyes. Rather than rushing off to gather supplies like I thought he might, he ripped a strip of material from his shirt and dunked it into the pool before handing it over to me.

'Thanks,' I mumbled.

The man who Fergus had tackled to the floor approached us, patting my patient's arm in a comforting gesture before sitting on the floor. I nodded in greeting.

'I'm Peter,' he said. 'Thank you for helping my people.'

I smiled and continued to clean the blood from the deep gash in the man's leg.

'What happened out there?' Robbie asked him.

'It was all so fast. The Riders descended on us from out of nowhere, and we had no time to run. It was a massacre all right, but this time something was different.'

'What do you mean *different*?'

'They were searching for someone in the village. They seemed to be sorting through the people before hacking them down.'

My pulse quickened as I worked on the man's injury and listened in on the conversation.

'Who were they looking for?' I could feel Robbie's eyes on me as he spoke as if silently blaming me for the gruesome end to this tale.

'Oh, they found her,' said Peter with a shake of his head. 'She never stood a chance. They just lifted her off the floor and threw her over the horse. I can still hear her screams.'

A chill shot up my spine. Did Crawford send the Black Riders after me? Did they take some poor girl thinking they'd found me?

'Poor Mrs Elrod, who knows what those demons will do to her.'

I dropped the damp cloth and grabbed Peter by his shoulders. My face was inches from his.

'Are you saying the Black Riders took Mrs Elrod with them?'

'Yes.' He nodded, looking between Robbie and me. 'That's exactly what I'm telling you.'

The fire crackled in the stone pit, and I shoved at it with a little more violence than was necessary. Newt was curled up in a ball snoring softly after crying himself to sleep, and the rest of us were too stunned to make conversation, so we sat around the dancing flames lost in our thoughts.

Halia had directed us to a safe clearing not far from the cave, where hundreds of people from the lower towns and the plains had made camp. At first glance, it looked like a thriving village nestled amongst the lush greenery of the trees. Upon closer inspection, you could see the rough makeshift beds and the haunted looks on the faces of the children. I walked through the settlement unable to miss the uncertainty in everyone's eyes.

It was clear from Peter's description that the Black Riders were under orders to take Mrs Elrod alive and we'd spent a good few hours speculating on why Crawford Reign would want the old woman.

'Maybe he's finally cracked and decided to punish her for the death of his mother?' Xander suggested.

'It wasn't her fault Lucy Reign died,' Fergus added. 'He can't hold her responsible for something that happened before he could even dress himself.'

'Well, she was on the plains when the Riders attacked recently, maybe they want someone to give them information, and she was just the unlucky choice.'

'I don't think it's that random, Xander,' Robbie muttered as he stared off into space.

Back and forth we'd gone thinking up every possible scenario, but if I was honest with myself, deep down, I knew why they'd taken Mrs E. Every resident in the Link knew how close I was to her. She was like family to me. Crawford Reign would have only needed to threaten one person, and they'd have spilt all my secrets. They were terrified of what might happen to them, and the young lord was an imposing character not easily fooled. I knew what he'd done. I knew, but I didn't have a clue how to tell my friends. He'd ordered the Riders to capture my friend so he had leverage over me.

I didn't want to think about what came next. Newt would freak out if I told him the plan that was formulating in my head right now. Xander and Fergus would probably have my back, but Robbie would look at me with judgement in his eyes, just like he had when I killed the guards in the moat, or when I threatened Theo's life to help us escape. I didn't know what he expected of me, but if he was looking for a gentle healer who needed him to protect her, then he was mistaken. I wasn't that girl.

The sky filled with a million stars, and I began to devise a strategy. The guards would be holding her either in the cells where Newt had been or in the tower they had taken me to. Both places had a connection to me and so, in turn, also had a connection for Crawford.

I was starting to understand his way of thinking. I'd rejected him, so he refused to release my brother; I'd done him harm by slapping him, so he held me captive; I'd escaped the tower, so now he had retaliated and taken my friend. It was my move.

Robbie interrupted my scheming thoughts by lowering himself down next to me and warming his hands on the fire.

'I know what you're thinking,' he said without looking at me, 'and the answer is no.'

I huffed and prodded the fire, causing sparks to shoot off in all directions.

'If he's taken the old woman it's for one reason only. He plans to lure you back to the city.'

'If that's his plan then it's worked because that's exactly what I'm planning on doing.'

He shuffled around until he was facing me, the glow of the fire lighting up one side of his face and casting shadows on the other.

'It's a trap, Maz. You can't play into his hands. If he gets you back inside the city walls, then he's won. He won't let you out of his sight again, and you'll be the Lady of Obanac before the day is out.'

I gasped. 'You know?'

'Of course I know, the entire realm knows. Crawford Reign has made it public that he's found a girl from the Link to unite the people just like his father did before him. Everyone knows it's bollocks and that he's got other plans for you.'

'What do you mean?'

'Sacrifice, Maz. We rescued those girls before they could become fodder for Cassias and his black magic, so he needs a replacement, and you're it.'

'How can I be the replacement? If I'm the Lady of Obanac then the city folk would expect to see me around at public events. He wouldn't be able to sacrifice me.'

'Oh, I'm sure he'd show you off for a while and act like the devoted lord but when the time came to raise the phantom then...' He dragged his finger across his throat to mimic my demise.

I looked away. There was a sliver of truth in Robbie's words. We had rescued the girls. Helene, Ami, and Tina had been destined for certain death, but they were now integral members of Halia's safe sanctuary. Were there other girls locked away in the bowels of the city? Or did Crawford Reign have his heart set on making me suffer his wrath?

'I can't leave Mrs Elrod in that place,' I whispered, tears springing up in my eyes.

'We'll get her out. Xander, Fergus, and me. You'll stay here where it's safe.'

'I don't need you to protect me,' I snapped. 'You weren't in the Link when Crawford came or when his guard dragged me to the tower. I was perfectly capable of looking after myself then.'

'I heard about Crawford coming to the Link,' he said. 'So, are you going to tell me what happened?'

Damn it. There was no other way around it. I had to tell him.

'He arrived the morning after we rescued Newt. I'd expected the guards but not him. He was...pleasant.'

Robbie raised an eyebrow and crossed his arms over his chest.

'I invited him into our hut and asked if he'd come to talk about releasing Newt, just like we'd rehearsed with Theo, but instead, he told me about the escape and asked if I knew who could have helped my brother. I feigned ignorance and shed a few fake tears but then before I knew it we were talking about his father and I was holding his hands.'

I blushed as I recounted the details to Robbie. He sat motionlessly but the crease in his brow deepened with every word out of my mouth.

I continued. 'I felt sorry for him; he seemed so lost. I just offered him some comforting words, but he must have taken that to mean something different and he...'

'He what?'

'He kissed me,' I mumbled, dropping my head and hoping my long red hair would cover the burning flames that lit up my face.

Robbie sprang to his feet and strode away into the tree line. Within seconds he returned with a furious expression etched onto his face.

'Why would you let him do that?'

I jumped up too and bunched my fists by my sides. How dare he assume I let the lord get away with anything?

'I didn't *let* him. He forced himself on me.'

Robbie looked like I'd just punched him in the gut. He took a step back, running his hands through his hair until it stood up in tufts.

'What else did he do to you?'

'Nothing,' I snapped. 'He made a quick getaway after I slapped his face.'

In that precise moment, I was tempted to re-enact the entire scene on Robbie. My blood was boiling as I tried to suppress the anger that bubbled just below the surface. Did Robbie think I would have welcomed an advance from such an evil monster?

Before I did something I would later regret I whirled on my heel and stalked off into the darkness. I needed some space.

I'd only gone a few paces before Robbie was in front of me, blocking my escape. He looked conflicted, like he wanted to tell me off but also hug me and tell me everything was going to be okay.

My shoulders relaxed as all the fight left my body.

'It was fine, Robbie. I'm fine. It was over in seconds. He took advantage, and I reacted. He threw me in the tower for embarrassing him and concocted a way to keep me prisoner in Obanac so he could continue to punish me forever. I get it. He's the Lord of Obanac, he's handsome, and he thinks every girl in the realm would want to be kissed by him, but not me.'

'You think he's handsome?'

I half giggled. 'Yes, but looks aren't everything. He's dead inside and has no soul, and he kisses like a toad.'

Robbie burst out laughing, and I smiled at the wonder of it. His eyes sparkled when he laughed, and the sound melted something in my heart.

'Kissed a lot of toads have you?'

I blushed again. 'Unfortunately, that was my first kiss, so I've got no point of reference. I know it wasn't pleasant.'

Robbie had stopped laughing and was studying me with a peculiar expression.

'What?'

He took a step forward until we were mere inches apart, tucking my hair behind my ear and trailing a finger along my jawline. My stomach flipped over alarmingly although it wasn't an altogether unpleasant feeling. Lowering his lips to mine, he kissed me, softly at first and then applying a small amount of pressure. It was nothing like my kiss with Crawford. This was tender and warm. There was no stubble scratching my face, and when Robbie encircled my waist with his hands I felt safe. I never wanted it to end.

Instinctively I wrapped my arms around his neck, pulling him in closer. Robbie's hands slid up my back exploring every curve. I was lost in the kiss. Lost in the moment. I was lost but didn't want to find my way back.

Before I was ready, Robbie broke away. His breathing was heavy as he kissed the end of my nose.

'Was that any better?' he whispered into my hair.

I laughed and lay my head on his chest.

'That was perfect.'

'I can't let you go to the city, Maz. I won't let Crawford Reign take you away from me.'

I understood. I never wanted to leave Robbie's side again, but Mrs Elrod needed me to save her, and I wasn't going to let her down.

'I know what might work in our favour. The night we rescued Newt the guards thought I was a boy. Even the lord asked me who the two men were that helped my brother. Let that *boy* save Mrs Elrod.'

ELEVEN

Robbie and Xander had wandered around the market square for two hours trying to find out as much as they could about Mrs Elrod's capture while Fergus and I prepared the weapons back at the mountain village. When the boys returned all they could talk about was the buzz in the Link and how, for the first time in their history, the residents of the lower towns were being invited inside the city walls.

'He's clever, I'll give him that,' Fergus said as he polished his sword. 'Crawford's making sure this is one trap nobody can resist. I mean, who doesn't want to see inside the city walls?'

'I don't,' I said bluntly as I stuffed my quiver with arrows. 'If Halia's vision was right, the wards around the city are to keep people in, not out.'

'Does that mean you won't be able to leave once you get inside?' Newt nestled himself next to me with a worried frown.

'Don't worry, kiddo, we'll be safe,' Robbie said, ruffling my brother's hair.

I shot Robbie a look over Newt's head. He didn't know that we'd be safe. He didn't know anything at all apart from why the lord was suddenly throwing open the gates to the city.

'I bet Mrs E loves all this fuss at her expense,' Robbie said in a strained attempt to ease Newt's worry. 'She was always telling us how much she wished she could go back inside those walls, and now she's being used as bait by her old friend's son. She'll be sitting by this fire chuckling about her adventure soon enough.'

Newt huffed and shrugged his small shoulders. Since we'd broken him out of the cells, I'd noticed how introverted he had become. Gone was the adventure-seeking little boy who would do anything to get into trouble with Robbie and his gang. I wanted that fun-loving and mischievous boy back, and I wanted him to live in a world where he was free of tyranny and fear.

'Do you really think Crawford would kill her?' asked Xander.

It's a thought that had been rolling through my mind since Peter told us about the Black Riders. She was an old woman who wouldn't harm anyone. Surely even Crawford Reign wouldn't hurt a defenceless resident of his realm?

'I hope not. Crawford's using her to get to me, so he's going to keep her alive until I turn up and offer myself as a replacement.'

'He's going to be disappointed when he gets four boys and a hail of arrows instead then,' Fergus said, nudging Xander and laughing loudly.

I smiled at my friends as I watched them prepare for battle. It was laughable to call it a battle when our plan was simply to infiltrate the castle grounds and free Mrs E. The murmurings in the Link pointed to the promise of a hanging in the city square, and I felt sick to my stomach that we might not get to her in time.

Robbie had outlined the rescue plan late last night around the fire while our friends remained oblivious to the kiss we'd just shared.

Neither of us had spoken about it, choosing to throw ourselves into the rescue planning and preparation. It felt nice to know that after all the name-calling, teasing, and mocking Robbie did have feelings for me. I realised that my determination to push him away and shield Newt from Robbie's influence was also a veiled attempt to hide my own emotions.

If we survived the day maybe we'd talk about what happened between us and where we went next, but if Crawford Reign got his way, by nightfall I could be locked in the tower and destined to be the Lady of Obanac for all eternity.

Robbie hadn't been joking when he told us the city gates had been flung open to the lower towns. I'd never seen anything like it. Market stalls lined the long track between the gatehouse and the main city gates, which stood wide open. Crowds of people bustled back and forth along the moat pass with free access into Obanac.

Dressed as pedlars the four of us wandered along with the throng keeping our hoods up and our heads down. Soldiers were dotted along the main road and positioned atop the castle walls. Scarface paced outside the courthouse as we approached the orchard.

'Fancy an apple?' Fergus whispered, digging me in the ribs.

I gave him a withering look as he chuckled and moved after Xander, who was a few steps ahead.

'Where's the main square?' Robbie asked as he sauntered alongside me. I marvelled at how calm he was. I was convinced that both Crawford and Cassias would know I was here because of the booming beat of my heart. The sound invaded my ears and drowned out everything else around me.

'It's up ahead and to the left by the main entrance to the castle.'

He nodded and moved away from me. The one instruction Robbie had given me was to try to blend in, and as I ambled along the same route Newt and I had followed at my blessing I began to wonder if blending in with the city folk was in my future.

Halia told me that the vision I'd seen in the pool was subjective and could be changed, but what if my destiny was written in the stars? What if I was supposed to stand with Crawford Reign and use my position as Lady of Obanac to help the people across the realm?

I rounded the corner then realised the stupidity of my own thoughts. There was no way I would ever stand beside Crawford Reign. Not in this lifetime or any other and the reason was displayed in front of me for everyone to see.

In the centre of the city square, a stage had been erected with a gallows and a hangman's noose. My stomach turned over as I saw my old friend slumped on the floor with a hooded executioner standing over her.

I stopped in my tracks, my entire body shaking. The instinct to rush to my friend's aid was overwhelming. Sweat coated my palms as I repressed the scream that bubbled up in the back of my throat.

I was on the verge of losing my mind when a strong hand slipped into mine and tugged me off the path behind a group of neatly pruned hedges.

'Breathe,' Robbie said, pulling me close. 'We'll get her away from here in one piece; I promise you that.'

I clung to him until the tremors in my limbs subsided.

'She looks so frightened,' I whispered.

He tucked my hair behind my ear and adjusted my hood so I was suitably concealed before leaning forward to kiss me gently.

'We can do this,' he said.

A short, shrill bird call filled the air, and we recognised it as Xander's signal that Crawford Reign was arriving. The crowds swelled as people jostled for a closer look. People from the Link and the other lower towns were congregating in groups and pointing at the gallows. The look of shock and surprise on their faces told me they hadn't been expecting to see Mrs Elrod at the foot of a noose either.

The elite guard marched from the castle doorway, flanking the Lord of Obanac. The city folk cheered and waved in delight, but the villagers from the Link fidgeted on the spot, their eyes darting around them as if anticipating danger.

Fergus and Xander took up their positions by a large statue of a young Davis Reign with a sword in hand. The sun glinted off the hilt of Fergus's dagger as he pulled his cloak tight around him.

I wiggled my bow out from under my green cloak and detached an arrow from the quiver I'd strapped to my body beneath my shirt. Within seconds I was armed and ready for action.

'Wait for my signal,' Robbie said as he stepped forward into the crowds and made his way to the front of the throng. I saw the top of his head as he broke through the swarm to stand alongside the gallows. If Mrs Elrod looked up now, she would see him clearly and know that all would be well, but the old lady's eyes remained downcast.

The sound of Crawford's heavy boots on the stage wrenched my attention from my friend. He sauntered to the centre and waved out at the gathered city folk, the sun highlighting the blackness of his raven hair.

'Welcome to Obanac,' he boomed.

The city folk cheered and waved their hands in the air.

'For the first time in history, I've opened the gates to our glorious city so that our neighbours and friends from the lower towns can join our festivities for the day.'

More cheering.

'However, I must report that not everyone from the lower towns has been so appreciative of our hospitality. Earlier today my guards found this woman stealing from the great hall.'

Shocked murmurs rippled across the crowd, and the city folk shook their heads in disgust. I scanned the sea of faces and saw people I recognised, friends and neighbours from the Link, exchanging worried glances. They didn't believe the story any more than we did. They'd heard Mrs Elrod talk about her fondness for the city and her time spent in Lucy Reign's employ. She would never steal from anyone. We knew the truth. We knew about the Black Riders and the trap Crawford Reign had planted for a red-haired girl from the Link.

'We don't tolerate this kind of behaviour here in the city, so there is no other choice but to sentence this wretch to be hanged.'

The city folk cheered as if watching a favourite sport. Nausea overcame me as the executioner dragged my friend to her feet and slipped the noose over her head.

I dragged my gaze away from Mrs Elrod to check that Fergus and Xander were in place. They both caught my eye and nodded. I looked out across the swarm of people for Robbie's head and saw him edging closer to the stage.

The executioner stood back and held the lever to the trap-door. One tug on the handle and Mrs Elrod would plummet through the hole in the floor breaking her neck in the process. He waited for the lord's signal.

Crawford Reign shook his head to show he wasn't quite ready for the grand finale. The executioner waited. The crowds waited. Crawford Reign waited.

His black eyes searched the hordes of people, looking for me. He was expecting me to come to him and give myself over to save my friend. Dread pooled in my gut as I realised he would never stop. If we managed to save Mrs Elrod today, he would take someone else tomorrow, and so on. What would I do if he took my brother again and threatened his life like this, or Robbie?

By now the city folk were growing restless and baying for blood. Struggles were breaking out between the well-dressed men of the city and the villagers from the lower towns. If someone didn't alter the status quo soon, we'd miss our chance, or worse, Mrs Elrod would die in the middle of a full-scale riot.

From my position, I could see Robbie was pinned back by the soldiers surrounding the stage, and Fergus and Xander were being pushed back by retreating villagers eager to leave the city and return to the safety of their own homes in the Link.

Crawford stood in silence glaring out at the crowd, his eyes as cold as flint. Realisation visibly dawned that I wasn't coming and with it his anger bubbled over into a screaming rage.

'Kill her!' he screamed at the executioner.

I'd fired the first arrow before he managed to reach for the lever, his wiry, hooded frame dropping to the floor in a bloody heap. The second arrow sliced through the rope, freeing Mrs Elrod. In the commotion, Robbie flung himself forward and dragged the old woman off the stage and into the startled crowds.

My third arrow I sent sailing into the wooden plinth inches from Crawford Reign's head. He yelped and shrieked at the guards to find the person responsible. I allowed myself a brief smile before breaking cover and rushing back along the path to the gatehouse.

We'd sent word to Theo, who had been given the task of distracting the guards once we made it to the gate. He was adept at getting anyone to do his bidding, and by feigning an injury, or bumbling at just the right time, he would allow us the time and space to slip away.

Fergus and Xander were way ahead of me as I permitted myself to be swept along with the villagers, who fought their way through soldiers and city folk alike to get to the gate. I kept my head down and my hood tight. As I pulled alongside the orchard, I glanced back to the square. The stage was empty, Crawford Reign no doubt hurried off to safety by his elite guard. Robbie was tearing through the crowds with Mrs Elrod bundled up in his cloak.

They passed me by, and I breathed a sigh of relief as they hurtled through the gate and out onto the track and the Link beyond.

Soldiers were shoving anyone from the lower towns out onto the moat road with such force that one man landed face first into the tar pit, and two men fell into the deep gorge, their cries muted only when they were impaled on the razor-sharp rocks below. Approaching the gatehouse, I spotted Theo's navy robes and made my way toward him. He would be able to clear a path for me as I fought against the tide of bodies.

Theo saw me and motioned for me to slip through a break in the defence that he created with a stumble over the hem of his cloak. I squeezed his hand as I flew past and had almost made it out from under the portcullis when Crawford Reign's booming voice cut across the cries and commotion.

'Bring the holy son to me!'

I faltered in my step and lurched to a halt. In the distance, Fergus and Xander were helping people clear the moat at the far end, safely outside the city's perimeter and wards. Robbie and Mrs Elrod weren't far behind them, and Robbie stopped briefly to check that I was safe and following close behind. His face crumpled when he saw something was wrong.

I spun on my heel in time to see two of the lord's elite guard drag Theo in front of Crawford Reign. I moved behind the lingering crowds of city folk, noting the presence of the occasional desperate-looking Link resident.

'Theodore, Theodore, Theodore.' Crawford paced back and forth in front of him with his arms folded across his chest. There was a tiny smirk dancing on the lord's lips, as if something he'd suspected for some time had been proved. 'Did my eyes deceive me, or did I watch my faithful servant assist an outlaw?'

'I don't know what you mean, my lord,' Theo spluttered.

'I'm fairly sure you do. I've been concerned about you for a while now, which is why I sent your father away. It's no good hiding behind the skirts of a parent, Theodore, especially a holy man who would be so disappointed in your actions. My sources also tell me that you have many friends in the mountains and out in the lower towns.'

'My lord, it's my job to work with everyone in the realm,' Theo protested, but Crawford cut him off.

'Work with them to what end though? I hear things, Theodore. Troubling things. My guards tell me you enjoy late-night visits to the cells. One specific cell if I'm correct. The same cell where a valued prisoner broke free.'

Theo's eyes widened as he listened to the accusations. Crawford Reign had been watching him for some time, and God only knew what else he'd seen Theo do. My pulse raced as I realised the magnitude of Theo's predicament. Did Crawford know how special Theo's friendship was to me? Had he found another victim to terrorise?

'You were there when that same prisoner escaped the city. You were busy distracting my guards then too.'

'I was shot!' Theo argued in his defence.

'Ah yes, but it was only a graze. Then you were also present when our future Lady of Obanac fled the tower after knocking you and another young soldier out cold. You understand the dilemma you've put me in, don't you, Theodore?'

'My lord, please believe me when I say I'm loyal to you and the city.'

'Liar! You consort with those creatures in the mountains, you plot against your lord, and you help outlaws escape my justice.'

The portcullis crashed to the ground behind us causing everyone present to leap out of their skin. Theo spun around to face the sound and when his eyes found mine in the crowd a light moan escaped his lips. At that moment I realised that he'd been prepared for this. He was prepared to accept his punishment if it meant we were all safe. But from the tremors in his hands and the slight shake of his head, he understood that both of us were now in grave danger.

Crawford noticed the change in Theo's stance and strode forward studying everyone who was assembled by the gatehouse. I knew he wouldn't know it was me unless I lowered my hood. To anyone else I looked like a boy in a dirty green cloak, dark trousers, boots, and a plain cream shirt. I bowed my head and waited, hoping he would grow bored of this show and let us all go. If he threw Theo in the cells for a few days, we would be able to break him out. It would be risky, but I knew we couldn't leave our friend behind. Halia would look after us all, and I knew she'd be pleased to see that Theo was safe.

Crawford spun away from us and returned to Theo's side. They stood eye to eye, and I wondered if the lord would offer some compassion for the sake of his holy man.

As we sucked in a collective breath and waited for the lord to inflict his justice an intense sensation of loathing washed over me. The skin on my arms puckered as if I'd plunged them into icy water. From beyond the bank of soldiers, Cassias stepped forward to shelter beneath one of the apple trees. My stomach lurched to see him out here in daylight, visible to everyone who took the time to notice. In his hand, he held a large purple crystal that pulsated with an eerie light. I recognised it from the vision in Halia's cave and fear pooled in the pit of my stomach. His eyes flared with fire, and within seconds Crawford Reign was snapping his orders.

'Guard! Cut our holy son's throat.'

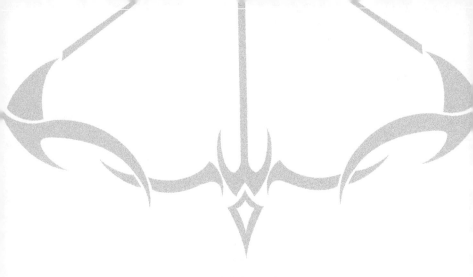

TWELVE

Theo struggled against his captors, crying out in alarm as Scarface pulled a long-handled dagger from his belt and grabbed him by the collar. Panic swirled around my insides as my mind raced with possible scenarios. Nothing would work. We were trapped and fighting against the lord's elite guard as well as the unnatural forces of an evil sorcerer.

I had two choices. I could watch my friend die a horrible death and probably die myself straight after, or I could hand myself over and hope that Crawford Reign would spare Theo. Either way, I was probably going to die, but I needed to hope that I could save my friend along the way. Whatever it was that Cassias and Crawford had in store for me would take time to arrange, and I had to trust that my friends would get to me before then.

As Scarface touched the blade to Theo's throat, I took a step forward.

'Stop!' I shouted, moving slowly through the crowd until I was almost in front of the lord and his elite guard. My hands shook as I came to a halt.

'No, don't do it,' Theo cried.

Crawford Reign glanced between Theo and the *boy* in front of him, confusion dancing across his features. I squared my shoulders, and the soldiers surrounding Crawford made ready to protect their lord if the strange newcomer launched an attack. In the distance, Cassias smiled.

I lifted my arms and dropped my hood.

Crawford took a step back, shaking his head as if trying to dislodge the image from his mind, a look of horror plastered across his face. I could almost see the pieces falling into place for him as I held his gaze.

'*You* are the outlaw?' He ran his fingers through his raven hair and paced back and forth. I hadn't expected him to appear so distraught at the thought of his lady being the Link rat that the city folk assumed I was. For a brief moment, I wondered if my indiscretion was enough to put him off, but I wasn't going to be that lucky.

'Take her away,' he growled, shaking his hands as if he could magically make me disappear. 'And take this traitorous boy too.'

Scarface grabbed my cloak, which fell open to reveal the quiver of arrows I'd strapped beneath. His scar stretched across his face as he smiled.

'What you got there?'

Everyone turned around at the sound of his voice. Crawford glanced back at us, noticing the weapons, and his body seemed to crumple in on itself. The clues were there for all to see. I was the outlaw who fired an arrow at their lord and helped save a suspected thief.

'Looks like you picked a proper feisty one here, my lord.'

Crawford ignored the remark and strode up so he was inches from me. Through gritted teeth he snarled at me, 'This changes nothing, Marianne. You are the one, and nothing you or your band of friends do will ever change it. Our fates are entwined and the harder you pull, the tighter the leash will become.'

What did he mean by *our fates are entwined*? I didn't have a fate and even if I did it certainly wouldn't be entwined with someone like him. Panic bubbled up in the pit of my stomach again, but Theo was in no position to offer me comfort this time. We were both being held by soldiers who were under orders to lock us up.

I caught Theo's eye and gave him a small smile. It was the only way I had to offer an apology. He smiled back, and I understood we still had our bond of friendship.

'Cassias, they're all yours,' Crawford hollered as he spun around and marched off in the direction of the castle with his guards in tow.

I was still reeling at his words when a deep rumbling vibrated across the open space. The remaining city residents had already fled back to their homes, which left everyone else to ready themselves for whatever was making that noise. As I looked out across the orchard, it began to wobble and shimmer. My vision faltered as if the world was tilting. Just like in Lucy Reign's bedroom a large portal ripped a hole in the fabric of our realm, and the Black Riders poured out of the swirling mass.

I pulled against the guards holding me, but they kept a tight grip. Theo was trying to wrestle with his captors too, but neither of us could break our bonds. I watched the deadly warriors circle us and finally realised how they were getting through the mages' wards out on the plains. Cassias had crafted a portal to send his demon army anywhere he wanted. Nobody stood a chance.

One of the riders reached down and grabbed my shirt, hauling me off my feet and into the saddle in front of him. A bone-deep chill emanated from him and I trembled in his grasp. Seeing the terror these riders caused when they trampled the plains was nothing compared to the sheer dread of being so close. Mrs Elrod must have feared for her life when they took her, and now we were in the same shocking situation.

We headed toward the floating portal and I glanced back through the portcullis to where our friends stood at the border of the Link. They looked helpless and defeated as my eyes locked with Robbie's. Xander was holding Robbie back preventing him from running along the track to the gate. There was a look of panic and desperation on his face, and it broke my heart. I hoped he would remain strong for Newt, and Mrs Elrod, and for the masses of people who flocked to the mountain village every day. I needed him to be a leader for everyone else so I could concentrate all my efforts on staying in control of myself.

Whatever happened, I had to believe that my friends would continue to fight for the people in the lower towns and I prayed that we would all survive what was to come.

The air was cold and static in the grey fog of Cassias's portal, leaving a metallic taste in my mouth. So many permutations of where it would take us spun through my mind that it made me feel dizzy. After what seemed like only seconds it spat us out in the bowels of the castle, which, upon closer inspection, was pretty much the worst option. How cruel to be so close to my friends and family and yet feel so far away.

Cassias was hunched over a large table littered with jars, papers, and crystals, oblivious to the Black Riders and their horses as they swarmed the cavernous room. The space stretched away further than the eye could see, disappearing into dark corners. The room had been chiselled out of rock, and I vaguely remembered my father telling me about the crypt and caves used by the phantom's army in the old days.

The rider dragged me from the saddle and threw me to my knees alongside Theo, who was shaking so much I could almost hear his teeth chattering. I gripped his hand in mine and squeezed his fingers. We were in this together.

'So touching,' Cassias said without looking up from his task. 'Touching yet foolish. The holy man will nourish you when you take on your role, Marianne. It might be wise to sever any attachments you may have to this boy.'

'What the hell does that mean?' I had to admit that the sorcerer freaked me out but I wasn't about to whimper and cry in front of him. He'd spoken in riddles when he'd visited me before in Lucy Reign's bedroom, and it appeared that this was just his way of communicating.

He looked up from the table and studied me with his bulbous red eyes.

'You have an important role to fulfil, Marianne.'

I laughed at the sorcerer's words. 'If you're going to start harping on about me being the answer to your prayers again, I'm going to request a change of room.'

'What are you doing?' Theo pulled on my hand.

'He's talking nonsense and expects everyone to understand. He told me I had a role to play and that I was powerful, but he's just a crazy old man who's been hanging out with his murderous army for too long.'

Cassias chuckled and the sound echoed around the chamber like a ghoul's whisper.

'You have no idea what your destiny holds, girl, but before the rise of the next moon you will be the most powerful being in the realm, and you will bow to me.'

Icy fingers circled my throat and I struggled to breathe. Black spots clouded my vision and I pitched forward bracing my hands on the floor. Theo wrapped his arm around me pulling me close.

'Leave her alone!' he screamed.

Cassias chuckled again and then turned back to his desk, flicking his wrist to release me from his spell. The air returned, and I gulped in great lungfuls of it while burying my head in Theo's chest. Whatever Cassias had planned for me, it wasn't something that a single bow and arrow, or the blade of a sword, could fix.

'Relax, boy; I have no plans to harm Marianne. On the contrary, she will soon be revered more than your father. She will be worshipped, celebrated, and most of all, she will be feared.'

'You're a madman,' Theo snapped as he clung to me. 'Nobody would fear Maz; she's pure of heart, unlike you and Crawford Reign.'

He spat the last sentence out as if saying Crawford's name caused him physical harm. He'd suspected for so long that something wasn't right about the young Lord of Obanac and current events proved him right.

Cassias watched the two of us as we huddled in each other's arms on the cold floor. He resembled a vulture studying its prey, patiently waiting for that final breath before ripping at the flesh.

'The entire realm will fear Marianne once the phantom consumes her, my dear boy, even you will turn your back on her once the power surges through her veins.'

My vision narrowed as the caves of the castle basement closed in on me. Dark spots swam across my eyes, and somewhere in the distance I could hear my friend calling to me.

The phantom's curse. Cassias and Crawford Reign planned to resurrect the phantom and use me as a host for the black magic. It was suddenly all so clear. The stories my mother used to tell me about Lady Lindley came to mind. She had been a young girl, like me, passionate about the realm and devoted to her people. The phantom had invaded her mind, body, and soul and turned her into a monster.

The army of the undead that I'd foreseen in Halia's pool wasn't rising on Crawford's command, they were following me.

'I will never let you resurrect that evil,' I recovered myself enough to yell at Cassias as he sorted through jars and potions set out on his desk.

My outburst went ignored by the withered sorcerer, and I turned my wide eyes on my friend. The look of panic on Theo's face didn't help to settle my nerves. A terrified scream rumbled up the back of my throat, but I managed to swallow it and take in a long, deep breath. I wouldn't let this be my fate no matter what Cassias said.

'We'll get out of here,' I whispered to Theo, grabbing his hands and squeezing them in what I hoped was a supportive manner. 'We won't let these men use me to bring about the destruction of our world. Not this time.'

Theo's eyes filled with tears but he blinked them away and gave me a sad smile. It was the kind of smile I gave my dying patients, the one that half reassured them that they weren't going through this alone, but also gave away the certain death that followed.

'Don't do that,' I said. 'This isn't how we die, Theo. We have a job to do, and I need you to stay strong.'

'A job? The only job you'll have when he's finished with you is to burn this world to the ground.' He inclined his head toward Cassias, who was busying himself with roots and crystals.

'That's not going to happen.' I sighed. 'I promise you this, Theo. I'll do everything I can to fight against the phantom and stay true to who I am.'

The cold laugh that echoed around the cave raised the tiny hairs on my arms. It was a sound of pure malice.

'Oh, my dear Marianne, you are so naive.' Crawford Reign floated into view wearing knee-high black boots over grey trousers. His white shirt was in sharp contrast to the black of his hair, which he had slicked back out of his eyes. 'You don't even know who you are, so how can you be true to anything?'

I pulled myself up on wobbly legs so I could eyeball the Lord of Obanac. I wasn't going to let him or his pet sorcerer break me.

'My name's Marianne.' I spoke loudly and with an inner strength and resounding calm that I'm not sure I believed. 'I'm a healer from the Link, daughter to Simon and Katlyn and sister to Noah Fitz. I'm a devoted friend to the villagers in the lower towns and the people out on the plains and in the mountains. I'm sixteen years of age and old enough to break my oath to you and the city. I reject your rule and stand up for the rights of the common people. I will...'

'You'll what? Kill me with one of your arrows, run me through with your sword, or get one of your outlaw friends to murder me in my sleep?'

I mentally kicked myself for not thinking up the last one for myself. It would have solved all our problems in one night.

'You think you're a healer, Marianne, but in truth, you're much more than that. I saw it in you the first day we met. You have mage blood running through your veins, and powerful magic like that can be bent and manipulated at will, but you need to know how to wield that power; isn't that right, Cassias?'

'Indeed, my lord. We were right, the girl is exactly who we thought she was and their feeble attempts to hide her in plain sight almost worked.'

Crawford chuckled. 'I knew it. All those years we've searched for and sacrificed young girls in the hope that one of them was her, and all the time she was just beyond the walls. The moment I kissed her and it felt so wrong I knew it was true.'

I faltered at his words, torn between confusion and anger. Although being kissed by this maniac wasn't the highlight of my year it still smarted to hear him say that my first kiss felt wrong. I shook it off and channelled all my thoughts into who they believed I could be.

'And who, exactly, do you assume I am?' I squared my shoulders in an attempt to appear aloof but inside my heart was threatening to break out of my chest.

'You're Lucy Reign's stolen daughter. You, Marianne, are my sister.'

I stumbled backwards into Theo, who reached out to steady me.

'That's the most ridiculous thing I've ever heard. My mother is Katlyn F...'

'No she isn't!' Crawford screamed, launching himself forward so he was mere inches from my face. 'Your real mother was Lucy Reign and your faithful friend, Mrs Elrod, who you so gallantly rescued from the noose today, was the one who stole you from our dying mother's arms.' His eyes were bulging and a vein in his forehead pulsed as he spat the words out at me.

'She was destined for greatness, our mother. Cassias had been preparing her to receive the phantom's gift but then she fell pregnant, and he had to wait. Wait until you slithered out of her belly. Father never appreciated what Cassias was doing, he never understood the glory and the power that the phantom could offer.' He took a step back, and I watched the emotion drain from his features. His cold black eyes gleamed as he continued his story. 'When our father discovered his dear friend feeding that special tincture to his wife he went into a vile rage, beating his three-year-old son, who was merely helping to comfort his mother as she took her medicine.'

At some point during Crawford's ramblings I'd covered my mouth with my hands to stop from being sick. It couldn't be true. I wouldn't believe this lie, and yet it explained why Mrs Elrod never spoke about why she left the castle or what happened to Lucy Reign.

The boy who Davis Reign beat would have been Crawford, my brother, if I was to believe what he was saying.

He continued. 'Cassias was the only one to offer me comfort when our mother took her own life. He was the one who cared for me and taught me how to rule this land, and he'll be the one to bring us back to glory.'

I didn't know what horrified me more, the fact that we were related, or that my mage magic could be my downfall. It was only then that I remembered something even more sickening.

'That's why you wanted me to stay with you in the city.' A wave of nausea rose up in me.

'Our blood bond is sacred, Marianne, and standing together as brother and sister we will feed the phantom and conquer all the world.'

I gagged and turned away to vomit, which made Crawford laugh even harder.

'Our mother thought she was saving the world by giving you away to her handmaid and killing herself, but she was only stalling the inevitable. Cassias knew that they couldn't hide you forever and that eventually you'd seek me out. We're bound together, Marianne. Our fates are entwined.'

It was too much to take in, and I struggled to process all the emotions that invaded my senses. My entire existence was in jeopardy as I tried to rationalise Crawford's words.

'You're a lying snake, and you'll do anything to try and break me,' I said, anger rolling around in my gut. My skin itched as if there were a thousand beetles trying to break through. 'My parents are Simon and Katlyn Fitz, and I was born in the Link.'

If I kept saying it over and over, it might make it true, but somewhere deep inside me, a switch had flipped. Understanding settled over me like a cloak, and all the jigsaw pieces fell into place. As a child, I'd dreamed of the city and living the life of a lady. To anyone else these would have seemed foolish fantasies but what if they were memories passed down from mother to daughter? I couldn't deny the pull I'd felt toward Crawford either as I recalled all the times I stopped my work to watch him walking along the castle walls, or when he left the city with his guards.

Our fates are entwined. That's what he'd said, but I also heard another voice, Halia's, which told me that nothing was set in stone and if I only believed in myself I could bring back the light. Was that my destiny? Had Lucy Reign given me away to protect me from the darkness that was growing in the belly of the city? Or had she hidden me away until I was ready to face that darkness head-on? Davis Reign hadn't listened to the warnings of his people, but Lucy had. She had been close to Mrs Elrod and would have taken heed of the whispers.

'My parents are Simon and Katlyn Fitz, and I was born in the Link.' I repeated the sentence over and over, getting louder each time until I thought the pulsating vein in Crawford's forehead might explode.

'STOP!' he screamed, grabbing my chin in his strong hand. 'You can try and placate yourself with lies, but I know the truth. Cassias knows the truth. Even your old friend Mrs Elrod knows the truth. Our mother thought she was sparing you from danger by giving you up and letting our father think you'd both died in childbirth. She was strong like you and fought against Cassias's magic for a long time, but she was also weak and pathetic, choosing to end her own life instead of embracing the power of the phantom.'

He released my chin and whirled around in a full circle, his fingers bent like claws.

'All that power and glory lies here within these walls, and all it needs is a host. You get that honour, my dear sister. Our mother's blood runs through you. Her mage blood.'

Theo finally stepped up and spoke, giving me time to slow my rapid breathing and distract me enough from the murderous thoughts I was having.

'You tried to use Lucy Reign as a host for the phantom?' He was ignoring Crawford and talking directly to Cassias, who was still mixing and tinkering with pots and potions.

He ceased his activities to answer Theo's question. 'Yes, she was a powerful mage as is most often the case with children from the Link. I helped to nourish her relationship with Davis, but I never expected them to be quite so...compatible.' He chuckled to himself. 'She was only ever meant to be a puppet, but instead she infected Davis with her pure light and turned him into a weak-minded leader. I tried everything I could to show him the way, but he discarded me and banished me to live out my days beneath the castle.'

'Davis Reign was good at discarding people,' Crawford snapped.

'My heart bleeds for you,' Theo mumbled.

'I've heard your father say that time is a great healer, Theodore, and they're wise words. I had all the time in the world to perfect my potions, find and build my army, and wait until she arose.' He pointed a wrinkled finger in my direction. 'Now we are ready to restore the realm to its former glory, and you two are going to play your parts.'

I screamed as two thick hands grabbed me from behind. The chills that shot down my spine confirmed my fears that the Black Riders were here to do their master's bidding.

'Enough talk. Shackle them both!'

I kicked and twisted my body to break free from the iron grip, but it was useless. As the soulless warrior secured the chains around my wrists, all the earlier bravado left me. I reached out for the white light within but only felt emptiness. There was no way we were getting out of this situation any time soon. Robbie didn't have a clue how to find us, and nobody within the city walls who had witnessed Cassias and his demon army would rally to our cause. I'd failed Newt, my friends, and the people from the lower towns. I was going to have my soul sucked out by the devil himself, turn everyone I loved into an undead army, and make the world bleed.

THIRTEEN

Sweat coated my face as I concentrated all my energy on fighting the bitter concoction that Cassias had forced down my throat. Cup after cup of foul-smelling liquid had passed my lips, and with each swallow, I was slipping further and further away.

Theo's frantic whispers washed over me as the cave swirled and sloshed in my vision. We had been chained to a wall side by side for what seemed like an eternity, but I was thankful that we were at least chained up together. If I was about to die, then I wanted a friendly face to be the last thing I saw.

'Keep fighting, Maz,' he urged. 'Remember who you're fighting for; remember Newt.'

Newt. My brother who wasn't my brother. I loved him as a brother and cared for him with everything I had in me. Keeping him safe had been my one responsibility in life, but I'd failed the second I stepped into the city on the day of the blessing. What was I going to tell him? How did I even start to tell the people I loved that I was related to the monster who was causing them pain and harm?

Cassias approached with another goblet and pressed the cold rim to my lips.

'No more,' I pleaded.

He smiled that wicked smile and prised open my mouth, emptying the contents of the cup down my throat until I gagged and choked on the festering tincture.

'It's done, Marianne. You're ready.'

My eyes grew wide as the withered sorcerer dragged a burning cage into view. The flames that licked the ironwork weren't like any fire I'd seen before. The fingers of orange and black wound themselves around the bars and hissed with every movement.

'What is that thing?'

'It's your new home, Marianne. Only hellfire can hold a pure mage's soul, and once the phantom consumes you, it will pull out your essence and dispense with your soul, placing it in its prison.'

My only hope was to convince him that I didn't have magic running through my veins, but in my heart I knew Cassias wasn't stupid.

'I'm not a mage; I keep telling you that, why won't you listen?'

'You might believe that lie, Marianne, but I can sense it in you. It's no matter to me if you've never awakened your power as it works in our favour. The phantom can't abide anyone who struggles. Lucy fought as did Lady Lindley before her, but with you, it should be an easy transition.'

I yanked on the chains that bound me as tears slid down my face. How was this happening to me? Halia had believed that I was the one to bring everyone into the light; if only she could see me now. My light had fizzled and died before it ever got going.

Resting my head back against the cold stone, I closed my eyes and tried to picture Newt and Robbie. Theo had spent all his energy talking to me about our friends, the Link, and the swelling numbers of villagers heading to the mountain region for sanctuary. He'd worn himself out trying to keep my spirits up and had nodded off with his wrists still shackled above his head.

As friends go, I couldn't fault Theo's loyalty. I'd shot him with an arrow and knocked him out with a chair leg, and he still tried to protect and save me. Robbie, Fergus, and Xander had all rallied around to help me rescue Newt with only a small amount of resistance, and Mrs Elrod had been by my side all my life, although now I understood why, and it wasn't because she was such good friends with my parents. If I was to believe Crawford's story, then Simon and Katlyn had taken me into their home at Mrs Elrod's request, pretending I was their own child to help cover my lineage.

For so long I'd thought I was alone and yet as I hung from the wall of a dank castle basement in iron handcuffs I realised that was never the case. I was surrounded by incredible family and friends who never turned their back on me no matter how dire the situation.

The sudden shift within me rose to the surface like I'd been submerged for a long time and had broken free. The air rushed into my lungs, and I gasped. Every fibre of my being vibrated as I woke up from what felt like a hundred-year sleep. My focus was sharper and the fear that sat like a boulder in my gut dissipated. Theo's soft snores filled the space around me, but there was something else in the air too, the tang of magic as a faint crackling emanated from the ends of my fingers.

Mage Hall had told me on many occasions that I held magic in my veins, and Halia had tried to help me find that power, but I'd dismissed all their teachings, choosing to believe that I was nothing but ordinary. Even though I had the red hair and bright green eyes which were the classic colourings of a mage, I still denied the heritage they wanted me to accept. Now, as the bright white light of pure mage magic flushed every inch of my mind, body, and soul, I knew the old man, Halia, and even Cassias had been right. I'd never been able to unlock it because my mage mother hadn't been alive to teach me. Lucy Reign had died trying to save me from this fate, and her actions meant that I never stepped into my authentic power—until now. I wasn't ordinary—I was extraordinary.

Theo's chatter about family, friends, and loyalty had unravelled the threads of sorcery and freed me, and as I breathed in the new light and let it consume me a plan hatched in my mind.

'No! Get away from her.' The sound of Theo's desperate sobs tugged at my heart and mingled with the urgent footsteps that echoed through the cavernous space. For my plan to work and be believed I'd employed all the teachings of being a healer and combined them with my newfound magical powers, however unstable they might be.

'I said leave her alone!' Theo shouted again.

'Shut it, boy,' snarled the guard standing closest to me. 'She's gone and there's nothin' you can do about it. We can leave her shackled to the wall if you want a rotting corpse as a roommate.'

The guards laughed as they set about freeing me from my chains.

Somewhere in the distance Crawford was screaming obscenities at Cassias for murdering his sister. I allowed myself a brief internal smile.

Dying was the easy part. Slowing my heart until it was on the verge of stopping had taken all my concentration and the best part of the night. Theo had stirred a few times but must have assumed I was asleep and returned to his slumber. Cassias checked in on me once early evening to anoint me with some god-awful oil that smelt of swamp water and burnt corpses. I didn't dare think about the process the old sorcerer had used to create such a potion.

Once he'd left, I set to work lowering my body temperature and slowing my pulse. I had to be careful not to go too far, or they would be burying me for real.

The pure mage magic allowed me to appear dead to anyone who checked my body. No pulse, no heartbeat, cold to the touch, and no breath. I knew this was breaking Theo's heart to think I'd died beside him but I needed his reaction to be genuine for the plan to work.

Crawford believed it, Theo believed it, and even Cassias, who had taken much longer to check me, now believed it. I was dead.

'How could you let this happen?' Crawford screamed in fury as he tore through the cave smashing jars and overturning tables.

The two guards assigned the task of releasing me lay me on a wooden table, careful to avoid the ire of the lord by being gentle with his departed sister.

'She was the key to everything, you fool.'

I heard the thud of someone being knocked to the ground and almost opened my eyes to witness the sorcerer's punishment. He had raised that small, broken boy to be the cruel and twisted man he was today and deserved everything he got, but before I could secretly gloat, Crawford screamed out in pain. Cassias was retaliating.

The Lord of Obanac was gasping for breath somewhere to the right of where I lay. The sight of his face turning purple and his black eyes bulging in fear flashed across my mind. Was that a vision or wishful thinking? Either way, if Crawford died, it would leave Cassias in charge of the realm, and I couldn't let that happen.

I had hoped to draw out the situation and wait until I'd been taken to the burial room in the church before bringing myself back to life, but from the explosive screams and clatter of broken furniture I needed to act now.

I flooded my body with white light and jumped down from the table giving both guards the fright of their lives. In the panic, I grabbed a sword from the guard closest to me and ran him through then whirled on the second and cut him down. I felt sharper, faster, and more in control than ever before.

Cassias released Crawford from his sorcerer's grip and flew at me in a wild rage. His black cloak billowed behind him giving the impression of a crow taking flight.

I held up my hand, and an arc of light shot across the cave knocking the old man off his feet. In that second I grabbed the keys to Theo's shackles and released him, urging him to run for the doors leading to the castle. Crawford had wandered in and out of these doors every day as I watched and prayed for an escape.

'You were dead!' cried Theo as I grabbed his hand and pulled him into a sprint up the stone stairs. Crawford had recovered himself enough to shriek orders at his soldiers.

Cries of 'Get after them! Capture them! I want her alive!' drifted up behind us.

'It was magic,' I said. 'I found my mage light, Theo, and you helped me find it.'

He grinned across at me as we took the steps two at a time. They seemed to go on forever then we eventually burst out into the great hall.

'Huh! Who would have thought that the realm's most dangerous sorcerer was living underneath the great hall?'

I chuckled at Theo's incredulous expression.

'Let's go!'

The last time I'd been in this room I was wearing a green dress and pretty shoes with an embroidered sash across my body announcing to the world that I was sixteen and a loyal citizen of the realm. So much had changed. The scared girl who entered this hall that day no longer existed. She'd died in the bowels of the castle and was reborn as a pure mage.

The bright sunshine hurt our eyes as we thundered through the main doors and out into the castle gardens. We'd had no concept of time when kept captive. The deep gloom of the cave did not indicate whether it was day or night. With the high sun overhead we knew it was noon but how many days had passed since the Black Riders had taken us was anyone's guess.

'This way!' Theo tugged on my hand to guide me down the steps and out under the arched entrance to the garden. The cobblestones didn't seem as bright as they had before. Perhaps I was seeing the city exactly as it was rather than how I hoped it could be.

Women and children squealed and jumped aside as we tore through the streets heading for the portcullis. I had to hope that Cassias and his Black Riders hadn't used that portal to block the entrance. My magic was new, and although I'd managed to knock the old man off his feet, it didn't mean I was strong enough to take on an entire soulless army.

The gatehouse came into view as we sprinted past the orchard and the courthouse. Murmurings and an unnerving commotion swept through the crowds who spilt out of their homes and businesses to see what was happening.

The sight of us must have been terrifying as we both wore tattered and dirty clothes and had raw sores at our wrists from the shackles. The city folk might have assumed we were escaped criminals if their favourite holy man's son wasn't one of the escapees. Although I never expected any of them to risk their lives to help us, I hoped none of them would be stupid enough to try to stop us.

My heart leapt as Scarface stepped out of the gatehouse and blocked our path. His grin pulled at the puckered skin on his face as he crossed his arms and waited.

'Going somewhere?'

I didn't blink or miss a step as I strode forward, flicking my wrist to send the big man crashing into the portcullis. His head ricocheted off the iron, and he dropped unconscious to the ground. Gasps and cries from the gathering crowds filled the air.

'Open the gate,' I told Theo, who rushed off at once.

'Don't fear me,' I shouted to the people filling the streets. 'I want to help you and the people beyond these walls. The Lord of Obanac plans to raise the phantom once again, and I need your help to stop him.'

Shouts of alarm floated on the breeze as the city folk listened.

'It's not true!'

'He wouldn't dare.'

'Have mercy, save us all.'

The glinting teeth of the portcullis began to rise, and the stench of the tar pit moat invaded my nostrils. Everything was much crisper now. I'd never noticed the stink before.

The gate opened an inch at a time behind me as I faced the swelling crowds.

'It's all true. Crawford Reign is not what he seems, and he's scheming with the sorcerer Cassias to bring about the destruction of our world.'

At the mention of the old sorcerer's name, a panic set in that sent the city residents into a crazed dash for freedom. En masse they pushed past me, running for the open gate and the moat bridge beyond.

'No! Please stop,' I shouted.

In a flash I remembered our earlier discussions about Cassias using the wards to keep the city folk trapped inside rather than protecting them from anything outside. As the first few people reached the walls, everything we'd feared came true. There was a bright explosion, and six men disintegrated as they tried to pass through the gate. The shimmering protection of the city's wards turned orange just like the hellfire that coated the cage I'd seen.

Cassias had altered the wards in readiness for the phantom's ascension. He'd told me that Theo would nourish me once I became a host, and now I understood what he meant. The people in the city were here to feed the phantom—here to feed me. They were breakfast, lunch, and supper neatly packaged and bound within the walls. Once the phantom rose up, it would devour the souls of everyone within its grasp, and the undead army would follow.

The portcullis was fully raised, and the passage between the city and the Link was wide open, but none of us could take it. We risked instant death if any of us tried to leave the city.

The orange glow that licked the city walls was a reminder that nobody was getting out of here alive, but right now that was the least of our worries as the sky began to spin and shift. The swirling grey portal ripped apart the orchard, and Crawford Reign sauntered out with Cassias close behind. The Black Riders were nowhere to be seen, and I wondered where Cassias had sent his army. I hoped that Robbie was ready for them if killing my family and friends was part of the sorcerer's plan.

'Did you honestly think I would ever let you leave Obanac again, Marianne?'

Crawford looked pleased with himself as he strutted around the courtyard. His officials and men of power cowered on the ground alongside the nobility, bakers, and servants, their faces pinched with dread at what the young lord may be capable of.

'It was a clever trick you played pretending to be dead, but it hasn't got you any closer to your precious friends. All you've done is open the eyes of all these people to the horrors that are about to befall them.'

He held his hands up to quiet the burst of screams and cries from the assembled crowds.

'My father loved every one of you,' he shouted above the din. 'He loved you more than he loved his own son and heir, and for that, you will all pay.'

As one, the crowd swarmed forward, their anger and fear powering them on. I could see it in their eyes and wondered if I should prevent them from reaching Crawford and tearing him limb from limb. Even before the conflicted part of my brain could answer, Cassias had swept them aside like he was cutting corn with a scythe.

It was never going to be a fair fight. The people of the city couldn't stand up against the great sorcerer, but I could. The crackle of pure white light flew across the courtyard striking Cassias square in the chest; he crashed to the floor in a cloud of dust.

The buzz among the crowds began to grow as they edged away from Crawford and the sorcerer to take up position behind me.

Out of the corner of my eye, I saw Lauren, the young serving girl who had brought me food and helped me escape when I was in the tower. She darted behind me.

'We're with you, my lady,' she whispered before melting away into the sea of hopeful faces.

Hope. It was a powerful emotion and one that, given the right leverage, could bring about immense change, lift the spirits of the downtrodden, and offer peace across the realms.

If I could harness the hope of these people, I could defeat the black magic that bubbled up in Cassias and infected Obanac.

Theo arrived at my side with a sword in his hand.

'Bit different from your usual accessories,' I teased.

'I think it suits me,' he said with a wink. 'And I think I'll need it if I'm to fight beside you.'

I smiled across at my friend. 'Until the very end,' I said.

'Until the very end,' he repeated.

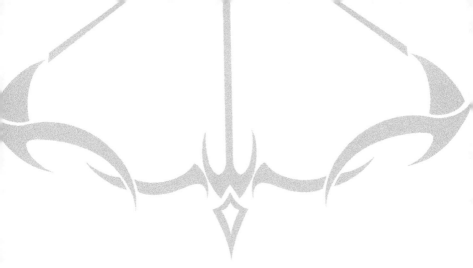

FOURTEEN

Crawford's elite guard spilt out of the courthouse and into the courtyard, standing behind their lord and master. Cassias had recovered himself enough and was on his feet and muttering under his breath. The purple crystal he held in his hand pulsed and wavered.

'What's he doing?' Theo asked.

'I'm fairly sure he's still trying to raise the phantom.'

Theo glanced across at me as if checking to see if I was still me and hadn't sprouted horns or begun breathing fire.

'My soul is still my own, Theo, don't look so worried.'

He chuckled but still mopped his brow with the tattered sleeve of his tunic.

'What now?'

'It's their move,' I said. 'I can fight fire with fire now, and that means Crawford can't just send his guards in to eliminate us.'

'So, it's a fair fight?'

'Something like that.'

The tiny pebbles on the floor began to hop and dance as a deep rumbling sound bounced off the city walls.

'Is this it?' Theo hissed. 'Has he raised the phantom?'

I had no idea what would happen if the phantom tore its way into this world, but I'm fairly sure it wouldn't come thundering over the plains and through the lower towns on the back of a horse.

'Black Riders!'

The city folk behind me cried out in terror as they spun toward the open gate. The soulless army was on the track crossing the outer limits. In no time at all, they would be over the bridge and would hack us down one by one.

Cassias's portal was no longer open, which meant the path to the courthouse was free and unguarded. I nudged Theo and edged him closer to the orchard.

'When I give the signal, run for the courthouse and take as many people with you as you can. Go down to the cells, and you'll find the way out into the crater. Use anything you can find to get yourselves out of here, but watch out for the wards. Hopefully, Cassias hasn't warded the lower levels.'

'I'm not leaving you,' he said, panic rearranging his handsome face.

'You're always right here,' I said, placing my hand over my heart.

Halia had been right about one thing. Once I started to believe in myself, all the pieces fell into place. I wasn't alone, even if my friends and family were scattered across the realms. They all held a portion of my heart, and they all stood beside me. They were my army, not the undead one I'd seen in Halia's pool.

'Now go!'

He hesitated for a second before launching into a run and calling for everyone to follow. Men, women, and children flocked after him putting their trust in the holy son. I half expected to be left to face the entire force of the Black Riders on my own, but when I turned to the gate, I was looking at a hundred men and women who had stayed behind to fight. Lauren was emptying the guardhouse of weapons and distributing them.

'It's hopeless, Marianne,' Cassias called out to me. 'You can't beat my warriors so why not put down your weapons and give yourself over to me?'

Lauren stood beside me, her bright eyes shining in the midday sunshine.

'Thought you might like this, my lady,' she said, handing me a bow and quiver of arrows.

'Just what I needed, thank you.'

I didn't need a physical weapon any more as I was now a living, breathing weapon of light but slipping the quiver over my shoulder and holding the bow completed me in a way magic never could. It felt like I'd come full circle.

'Be ready!' I shouted to the makeshift army as the first of the Black Riders crossed the bridge.

The sound of so many horses' hooves thundering across the wood was deafening, and the vibration rising from the ground tore through my chest. I'd seen these monsters in action and didn't hold out much hope that my small band of men and women could stand against them.

My magic sizzled beneath my skin, but I didn't have a clear shot at the riders as they pounded the floor growing ever closer. If I could create a space, I might be able to do some real damage to their numbers and give us a fighting chance.

I scrambled through the crowd that stood in defence of their home. They had lived under the rule of a sadistic lord for so long, but now I saw passion and determination etched upon their faces. I'd dismissed the city folk as lazy, pompous, and weak, but I'd been wrong. They were as devoted to their homes and family as I was to the Link and Robbie was to the plains, and they deserved every chance to protect their loved ones and create a happier and safer life for themselves. The Black Riders, Cassias, and Crawford Reign stood in the way of that dream, but not for long.

I'd watched the Black Riders sweep across the plains like a plague as they hacked and sliced at anyone in their way, but the warriors who approached held their swords low and slowed to a trot as they entered the gates. Something was different. I glanced back at Cassias to see if he was using sorcery to manipulate his warriors, but he looked as startled as I was.

The lead horseman pulled on the reins, bringing the army to a halt just inside the gate. A hundred of the city folks' swords pointed at him as he swung off the horse and landed heavily on the ground. He was big and brawny, and towered over the men and women who had bravely stood against the tyranny of the lord, his sorcerer, and this unholy army.

'Hey, Maz, how's it going?' The Black Rider unclipped his helmet and slipped it off. Xander's cheeky grin greeted me. 'We thought you might need some help.'

The rest of the Black Riders dropped from their horses and shed their masks revealing Fergus, Ely, Peter, and Helene. More of them poured into the city and were given a hearty welcome.

I didn't know how they'd defeated the Black Riders, but from the exhaustion wrinkling their brows and cuts and bruises on their faces I assumed it had been a tough fight. Robbie was heading toward me from the back of the group, his hair pulled back into a ponytail to keep it out of his face. He was smiling despite the blood pouring down his cheek from a long, angry gash. I thought I'd etched every detail of his face into my mind but as I watched him approach I realised I'd underestimated my own memory. Robbie was like a beacon of light in a dark storm, he was so handsome, and his eyes lit up as he spotted me. My stomach lurched as he reached my side and kissed me.

'Get away from her, outlaw!' Crawford burst forward in a fit of jealous fury, his elite army raising their weapons and readying themselves for the fight that was inevitable.

With a wave of my hand, the lord dropped to his knees.

'That's new,' whispered Robbie.

'Just a little something I picked up in the sorcerer's dungeon.'

'You'll pay for this, Marianne,' Crawford spat. 'Kill them all!'

The elite guard surged forward, and we burst into action. Robbie drew his sword, engaging with two soldiers who attacked from the right. I fired arrows into the advancing guard, their bodies dropping mid-run.

Over the heads of the advancing army, I spotted Crawford and Cassias skulking away, heading back to the castle.

'We need to stop the sorcerer,' I shouted across the noise of battle.

Robbie signalled to Fergus, who broke rank and took a handful of fighters with him. They scaled the embankment and circled behind the castle, cutting off Crawford's escape route should he try to get away. No doubt Cassias would slink back into his cave and try again to raise the phantom.

I made a path through the guards and ran with Robbie toward the front of the castle. Whatever happened I needed to stay far away from the flaming cage so my soul remained where it should be. Neutralising Cassias was the mission but if I had to kill Crawford, my brother, to achieve that goal then so be it.

The door to the great hall stood ajar as we crept inside. My arrow was poised ready to fire should any of Crawford's soldiers be waiting for us, but the hall was empty. The small wooden door leading down to Cassias's cave was shut with a black bolt across the top. If they hadn't gone down to the basement, where on earth could they be?

'Stay alert!' Robbie whispered.

I nodded and tiptoed further inside. It seemed strange to see the hall this way. It looked cold and uninviting unlike when the room was full of tables and people chatting and laughing as they waited for the blessing. That day seemed like an eternity ago, but I couldn't regret ever stepping inside the castle walls as those actions guided me to the person I was today. I'd embraced my power because I'd been forced to do so. Survive and thrive, that was what I'd told myself when I'd been chained up deep below these very floorboards.

Saving Newt, Mrs Elrod, and the faithful people of this realm was my main priority, but first I had to neutralise the threat that hung over all of us like a storm cloud.

A flash of purple caught my eye, and I swung my bow in that direction. Instead of finding the enemy, I saw Cassias's crystal lying on the ground.

In his haste to escape, he must have dropped the precious stone. Snatching it up from the floor, I stared into its milky shell. A tiny image swam in the surface of the stone, a picture of the castle walls and the orange glow of the wards.

In one smooth motion, I smashed the crystal hard against the ground, watching it break into a million tiny slivers. There were no windows in the great hall for me to see if the wards had come down, but in my heart I knew. The faint humming that had invaded my mind since I'd been here ceased and I realised that I'd been able to sense the magic all along. It was gone, and there was only silence. The wards were down and the people could escape.

'They're not here,' Robbie said, lowering his sword.

'Fergus might catch them if they try to leave from the back of the castle,' I added, suddenly worried for my friend. 'We need to help them.'

Before I could dash off to help our friends, Robbie grabbed at my arm.

'Wait!' His eyes were shining as he looked down at me. 'I just need a second to look at you and make sure you're real.' He chuckled, and I couldn't stop the smile that tugged at my lips.

'I'm fine, Robbie. When this is all over, I'll tell you everything, but for now I need you to know that I'm okay.'

He leaned in and kissed me gently on the lips. Everything disappeared for those few seconds, and it was just the two of us.

'You have no right to touch my sister!' Crawford's scream broke into our moment, and we jumped apart.

Robbie glanced across at me, his eyebrows so high they disappeared into his hairline. I didn't have time to explain that now so waved my hand to dismiss it as the ramblings of an unstable boy.

'It's over, Crawford,' I said. 'Your sorcerer is equally matched, his soulless army defeated, and your people know your plans to destroy the realm. You're finished.'

From behind one of the tapestries hanging on the wall, Cassias moved into view. His hood was up, covering his bald head and masking his face, but I could still see the sharp glow of his eyes. He clapped his hands and the sound echoed like a peal of thunder across the sky.

'You're so right, Marianne,' he hissed. 'It *is* over.'

The sorcerer circled his hands, and a large orange orb appeared between his palms. He was muttering words I couldn't understand, and dread trickled down my spine like icy water.

'We need to go,' I whispered, pulling on Robbie's hand.

As one we turned and ran for the door, bursting through the entrance and spilling outside into the sunshine. The sounds of metal against metal and bloodcurdling cries filled the air.

'What's going on?' Robbie asked as we hurtled through the herb garden and into the main courtyard.

'Cassias is raising the phantom, and he's decided to assign me as the host.'

Robbie came to an abrupt stop in the middle of the path, and I had to skid to a halt further along.

'We don't have time to discuss it,' I said, unable to hide the urgency in my voice. 'If Cassias raises the phantom and I'm still here, I don't think I'll be able to fight it and...'

'You'll destroy the realm,' Robbie finished for me.

'Yes, pretty much.'

'How is that possible? You're from the Link, and the other women who've been used as hosts were ladies of the realm.'

'There's no time, Robbie. We have to move, now!'

'No! Tell me, Marianne. What's going on?'

I rested my hands on my hips and circled toward him, my forehead creasing as annoyance bubbled to the surface.

'I *am* a lady of the realm. You were right all along. Lucy and Davis Reign were my real parents, but Mrs Elrod helped Lucy to hide me in the Link so they couldn't use me to raise the phantom.'

Robbie's mouth hung open as he listened to my babble. I was tempted to laugh, but the seriousness of the situation stopped me.

'Only Mrs Elrod knew the truth, but Cassias suspected that I was out there and that's why they've been taking girls from the blessings and massacring our people on the plains.'

'Well I'm glad to hear you say *our* people,' Robbie said with a smile. 'Are you still my Marianne?'

'Always,' I said with a twinkle in my eye. 'But you can call me my lady.'

Robbie burst out laughing and trotted up to my side. 'Never gonna happen!'

A booming sound filled the air and wrenched us from the moment. The sound of swords clashing halted and everyone in the courtyard, friend and foe, looked to the heavens.

Black clouds rolled overhead like swirls of fog, and lightning fractured the clouds. Although the sky was awash with churning shadows, it was the sounds that carried up from the earth that caused my blood to freeze.

From beneath the cobblestone paths that wound through the city a roar broke through the silence. It was a sound of pain, horror, and violence. A sound of pure evil. The motionless warriors who occupied the city streets and courtyard lurched into action. Crawford's elite guard swarmed forward alongside the men and women of the city and the fighters from the plains, all heading for the gate and the Link beyond.

They surged through the portcullis and across the bridge, and I breathed a sigh of relief that breaking Cassias's crystal had indeed dropped the warding.

'Run!' Robbie shouted over the rising screams and cries.

We rushed to the gate, helping anyone we could along the way. Bodies littered the streets, and my chest felt heavy at the loss of life, but if I didn't get clear of the phantom, the streets would run with rivers of blood, and the dead would rise as an unstoppable army—my army.

Robbie had reached the gate and was helping a young man to his feet. I sprinted after him. A faint whimper to my left distracted me and I spotted Lauren cowering beneath a broken earthenware pot. I ran back to where she had hidden herself.

'Lauren, come with me.' I held out my hand for her.

'I'm so scared,' she whimpered.

'So am I, but we'll do this together, okay, you and me.'

She wiped at her grubby face and gave me a small smile.

I reached forward and grabbed the young girl's hand as she extended it out to me. We ran for the gate as the ground behind us broke apart and the phantom burst through. Debris careered across the courtyard knocking us both to the ground.

'Marianne!' Robbie's cry ripped a hole in my heart as I watched the outer wall of the castle crumble and fall cutting us off from each other.

'We can't get out.' Lauren's tiny voice was full of panic, and I pulled on all my inner strength to stay calm for her.

'It's okay; we'll find another way.'

I had no idea if there was another way out, or if either of us would make it out alive, but I had to hold on to hope. I also didn't want to look behind me, but the desire to see the phantom for myself was too much.

Pulling the small girl to the rear of me, I rolled toward the crater that now sat inside the city walls. Smoke billowed into the sky as the dust from fallen buildings coated everything in its way. My vision was sharper now, and I was able to see through the smog to the centre, but what I saw there broke apart my resolve and allowed terror to flood all my senses.

The phantom was immense. A swirling mass of black and red. It shifted and changed as I watched, becoming a towering monster with muscular arms and a horned head. Its eyes blazed with hellfire as it hungrily surveyed the city. Sweeping forward it grabbed two guards from the floor turning them to ash as the beast inhaled their essence.

Lauren screamed and buried her head into my side, clinging to me like Newt used to do when he'd had a bad dream. Newt. If I didn't survive this day, my brother would die along with my friends, and I couldn't let that happen. I flexed my fingers and felt the mage magic flowing through me. I channelled all the memories of my family, all the stolen kisses I'd had with Robbie, and the laughter I'd shared with my friends. The pure mage light pulsed within me, and I smiled to myself.

From within the settling dust, I spotted Cassias and Crawford next to the phantom. Cassias stood with his arms outstretched as if in worship to the beast, and Crawford knelt before it surrendering his soul to the devil himself.

I glanced back at the rubble that was once the outer wall; from beyond it I could hear scraping and raised voices. My friends were trying to break through. They were clawing at the rocks and digging their way to us. I smiled at the vision that popped into my head. Xander picking up huge boulders and hurling them into the tar pit, Fergus ordering everyone else around and Robbie on his hands and knees tearing at the rocks. I didn't know if they'd get to us in time, but I wasn't going to go down without a fight.

'I refuse you access to my soul,' I shouted up at the swirling mass of muscle and fire that blocked out the sun. The phantom swung its head in my direction and I shuddered as its eyes found mine. The same fire that clung to the soul cage burnt in the monster's eyes and I was once again reminded of the vision from Halia's pool.

'She is your vessel,' Cassias said, pointing at me with his gnarled fingers.

I summoned the mage magic up through the floor calling on all the mages that had gone before me and whose bones and blood now occupied the earth. The power rushed into me and like a bolt of lightning from the heavens I sent the light of a hundred mages hurtling across the courtyard to hit Cassias full in the chest. The sorcerer remained standing as the magic ripped out his heart, leaving a gaping hole in his chest. The look of shock and surprise etched onto his withered face made his demise all the more satisfying.

Crawford watched his mentor and friend crumple to the ground before turning his black eyes on me.

'Sister or not, you'll pay for what you've done. I will control you and force you to kill your friends, and you will be powerless to do anything about it.'

His face was twisted into pure hatred, and I marvelled at the fact that we were both born of the same parents. He had been denied love, and it corrupted him beyond redemption. His outburst toward me hadn't gone unnoticed by the demon that loomed above him, but he was too slow to act as I screamed out in warning.

The phantom curled its giant claws around Crawford Reign, and I watched in horror as his body ignited. He withered and kicked as he burnt alive in the beast's grasp. His screams sent tiny vibrations through my body and enabled my mage magic to unlock his childhood memories so that I could snatch them from the ether. Pictures of a small boy running through the orchard with a smiling Davis Reign giving chase, being tucked up in bed and kissed tenderly by a loving father, and of our mother cradling a newborn as Crawford looked on with wide eyes. Finally, I saw the man he was today, but without the cold exterior of a haunted childhood. Through the swirling mass of fire I propelled my mage magic and tore a hole through the darkness. There was a time in his life when he was loved and maybe now, at the end, he deserved to find peace again. Gifting him with a passage to the next world was all I could offer. He smiled at me before walking away into the light. He was free and as the image of him disappeared the screams ceased.

'Are we going to die?' Lauren whispered as we watched the Lord of Obanac turn to ash.

'Not today,' I said.

The phantom roared again and shimmered in the failing light of the day. I glanced back at the wall and saw the chink of light from the other side. They had almost broken through.

'I need you to help move the stones, Lauren,' I said, herding the young girl toward the rubble. 'Help them move the rocks and then you can escape.'

She rushed off to the wall but stopped and turned around slowly.

'You mean so that *we* can escape, don't you?'

I smiled down at her and nodded. 'Of course.'

I had no intention of leaving this city while the phantom was alive. Cassias was dead, so I could only hope that whatever spell was needed to extract my soul had also died with him, but I didn't know if the phantom itself was capable of taking me over and devouring my being. The monster lurched forward. I was about to find out.

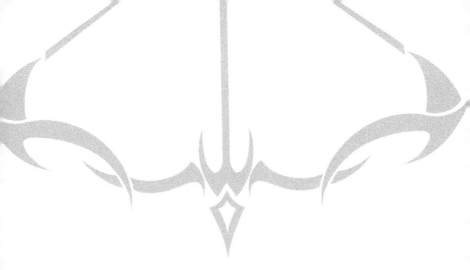

FIFTEEN

The beast's gigantic claws closed around me as I coated myself in the protective bubble of pure mage magic. Unlike Crawford Reign, I didn't burst into flames when the beast grabbed me; instead it was like wading through a fiery sandstorm with my magic keeping the flames at bay.

Although I was protected physically, I couldn't say the same about mentally. The visions rolled through my mind on a constant loop, draining me of my hope, determination, and fight. I saw Lady Lindley as clear as if she was standing beside me. Her bright hair was alight with hellfire, and her eyes were burnt to black holes. She was fighting her kin with a bloody sword, her undead army at her back. I could feel the raw power running through her and sense the greed for more. The vision shifted to another woman with hair as red as the sun. She was older than Lady Lindley but just as beautiful. A crown sat on her head as she looked out over a crowd of smiling faces. I was seeing the city as it looked centuries ago before the phantom destroyed our world. The image shifted to show the red-haired queen clawing at her throat, a fallen cup at her feet. In the background, a sorcerer skulked in the shadows.

The queen convulsed when the darkness of the phantom's curse devoured her.

Woman after woman fell to the curse as the vision spilt its secrets. The phantom was older than time and had devoured our world over and over.

My resolve wavered, but then I noticed something in the distance. A pinprick of light in the mass of blackness and fire. With everything I had left within me, I hooked onto that light and concentrated. It was like finding water in the desert.

Faces swirled into view. First was Lady Lindley, then the red-haired queen, but this time they weren't corrupted by the phantom's curse. They were bathed in the pure light of mage magic, and each face that formed in my vision was speaking my name.

'Marianne. Marianne. Marianne.' They repeated it over and over until it sounded like a loud cry.

Within the core of the darkness, I'd found the light, and I wasn't alone. The women who had been consumed by evil had come through the ordeal and were here with me. They died and found peace in the unity of their sisters, but their souls remained trapped for all eternity to watch yet more women fall to the phantom's curse. They stood in a circle around me, holding hands, the bright light flowing like a river around them.

My mind played out the vision and I began to understand what they were asking of me. United they stand. As one. Wasn't that what Halia had said to me back in the mountains? Unite the people.

My body physically jolted, and I tumbled to the ground. The vision cleared and I was back in the courtyard, released from the phantom's fiery grasp.

Rubbing my face to clear the sweat from my eyes, I looked around at the swarms of people who were rushing around me. The phantom was bellowing above us as wave after wave of arrows penetrated its sides. Devouring the guards and Crawford Reign had given it form, and that meant it could be harmed.

Hundreds of people poured through a newly created hole in the city wall. Robbie reached down and plucked me from the ground, dusting me off and giving me a beaming smile.

'You are one tough lady,' he said, handing me a sword. 'Now, let's finish this.'

I rounded on the phantom, backing away just enough for it to notice me. Those fiery eyes found mine, and a wave of heat surged over me as its claw swept forward once again. This time I was ready for it and coated the blade of the sword with mage light before sliding it into its palm as it reached for me. The horned creature gave an unearthly scream, and everyone stopped moving as one.

'Everyone hold hands,' I cried, pushing Robbie closer to the soldier standing next to him. They looked at me as if I'd gone a little crazy but did as I asked.

One after the other, men, women, and children grasped the hand of the person next to them, linking together like a human chain. In the distance, Theo and Lauren clung to each other; Xander, Helene, Fergus, and Ely clasped hands with city folk and some of the elite guard. It swept over the courtyard until every single person was holding onto the next one.

The phantom, recovering from the sting of pure white magic, rounded on me as I stood in front of the thousands of people who had flocked to the city. The thousands of people united as one.

It lowered its gigantic head, and the smell of death and decay poured from its mouth as the beast roared. I stood my ground, holding my sword in my right hand and with Robbie's fingers entwined in my left hand.

The phantom grabbed at me with its good hand, and once again the bubble of white mage magic protected me. I extended the protection to cover everyone in the vicinity as the hellfire spilt out into the crowds.

Without wasting any time dwelling on the darkness and that feeling of hopelessness that clawed at me as the phantom tried to take me over, I searched for that pinprick of light. I knew what I was looking for, or rather, who I was looking for.

The women stood together hands still clasped in unity as I dropped my sword and reached for Lady Lindley. She slipped her hand into mine, connecting us all with the power of the pure mage magic. It swept along the line igniting every single person that was linked to the next with white light. From within the darkness, the phantom shrieked as we all clung on to one another.

My body was buffeted as the beast fought against the overwhelming power of the light, but in the end, we were too strong, and we crashed to the ground as the phantom exploded in a ball of flame.

Nobody dared let go of the person next to them as we all watched the immense monster burn up from the inside. Its horned head melted and collapsed inside itself and the swirling darkness dissipated as the body and arms turned to ash. The phantom disappeared before our eyes with a deafening roar.

The air settled to leave a crisp dusk sky peppered with stars and I looked across at Robbie, who was still clinging to my hand.

'We did it,' I whispered. 'We killed the phantom.'

Soft murmurings carried along the line as everyone realised what had happened. Carefully, people disentangled themselves from their neighbour, almost afraid that the monster would return once they let go.

'Maz...' Robbie was looking off into the distance, and when I followed his intense stare, I saw them. They stood side by side dressed in white robes, their faces so pale they looked see-through.

'Thank you, Marianne.' Lady Lindley stepped forward and the gathered crowds gasped. 'You've freed us all from the phantom's curse.'

I bowed my head to each of them in turn.

'It was you who gave me the strength to beat the creature,' I said.

Lady Lindley chuckled and it sounded like a musical bell. 'You've always had that strength inside you, Marianne, you just needed to believe in yourself to set it free.'

The group of women, who had been through so much terror and heartbreak at the hands of the phantom, began to fade. Their shapes swirled and melted into the night sky, and we all watched in wonder as a shaft of light swallowed them up. Before the light closed, Lucy Reign smiled across at me, raised her hand in greeting, and pressed it against her heart. Power surged in my chest and I placed my hand over my own heart in turn. It was over in a second, but the connection to my birth mother filled me with such joy that I couldn't stop the tears from falling.

'Don't cry,' Robbie said, pulling me into a warm embrace. 'It's over; everything is going to be okay.'

He mistook my tears for something else, and I let him. Seeing my birth mother was something I wanted to keep to myself. A private memory that I would hold dear forever more.

'So, what now?' Xander asked as he wandered over to where we stood, Fergus sauntering up behind him.

'I think I know someone who'll have the answer,' Robbie said, nodding his head in the direction of the wall.

I looked over at the great hole where the gate used to be to see Theo embracing his father. The holy man stood before the immense crowd of people. Travellers, merchants, and soldiers from across the realm milled around behind him. He'd brought an army of his own home to Obanac.

I rushed to my friend's side and flung myself into his embrace.

'You did it!' he cried, beaming at me from beneath the dirt and soot that covered his face. 'You defeated the phantom.'

'I couldn't have done it without you, Theo.'

He blushed and kicked at a stone on the floor.

'All I did was hang from a dungeon wall and babble for hours until you pretended to die. You did all the hard work.'

I chuckled and gave him another tight hug. No matter how modest he was, we both knew what he'd done. If I was truly honest, we'd saved each other.

Theo circled toward the holy man and ushered me forward. 'Marianne, I'd like you to meet my father.'

I took the holy man's hand and smiled up into his warm face. He'd had a calming effect on me the day of the blessing, and that feeling re-emerged now as he shook my hand.

'I've heard so much about you, my dear, what you've done here today will be remembered and celebrated for generations to come.'

'Father, tell her what you did.' Theo was jumping up and down on the spot like a five year old, and it made both of us chuckle to watch him.

'Ah yes, well, I heard of Obanac's demise from a travelling merchant who told me about Crawford Reign's madness. I'd been worried about him for some time and knowing that Cassias was still alive just amplified those worries.'

His gaze drifted to the sky as if he was picturing the two men who tried to bring down the realm. He was an old and wise man and not someone to rush so we waited patiently for him to start talking again.

'Terrible business, really, but as I was on my pilgrimage, I began to hear stories about missing girls and soulless warriors. Theodore had tried to warn me before I left but I'm sorry to say I'd dismissed his concerns.'

He patted his son on the back by way of an apology.

'As I went from town to town I found so many people who had been torn from their families and scattered across the realm. I also met a lovely couple who told me an interesting tale about a stolen baby and how she was the saviour of the realm. I'm sure you can imagine my reaction...' He laughed to himself. "How absurd. We don't need a saviour," I thought, but then the stories kept coming, and I finally understood.'

'And...' Theo was beside himself as his father took his time telling me the news.

'And so I brought them all home.'

I studied the holy man for a moment expecting him to keep talking but he just stood there smiling at me. Theo was also smiling at me. There was clearly a punchline to his story, but I feared I'd missed it.

'I'm sorry,' I said. 'I don't understand.'

Theo exhaled, throwing his hands into the air.

'He brought *everyone* home to Obanac, Maz. Everyone!'

'Marianne!' A cry from behind us sent an electrical charge down my spine. I whirled around to see my parents rushing toward me with Newt clinging to their hands.

'Everyone's come home,' Theo repeated with a grin.

Children and parents, friends, lovers, and neighbours were reunited across the city as they poured through the broken walls. Davis Reign had fractured so many families when he banished them from his protection, but Theo's father had rounded them up and brought them home. I knew that the realm was going to be okay in his hands.

Rushing into my mother's arms brought all the happy memories I'd repressed over the years flooding back. I remembered the stories she told me, the herbs and spices we used at the stove to prepare Father's favourite meal, and the lessons she taught that helped me evolve as a healer.

I breathed in her scent and vowed to never forget what this moment felt like.

'I can't believe you're here,' I said between sobs.

She stroked my hair and peppered my forehead with kisses. Her face looked thinner than I remembered but her smile was still the same.

'We heard the rumours about Crawford's plan to install a girl from the Link as the next Lady of Obanac and I knew he must have found you.' She wiped my tears away with her thumb. 'It was my job to keep you safe from harm all those years and I failed you.'

'You never failed me!' I cried, burying myself in her embrace again. 'Crawford told me everything. I know that Lucy and Davis were my real parents, and I know that you risked your lives to protect me. You didn't fail me, Mum, you loved me with all your heart and that made me strong.'

'When the holy man found me on the road I was overjoyed. He'd already found your father and reuniting with him was the best moment of my life—until now.'

We clung to one another and let the tears of joy and relief flow. All around us people were reuniting with loved ones and the energy of everyone's happiness surrounded us.

My father tugged me gently from my mother's arms.

'My turn,' he said with a grin.

I giggled and flew into his arms. All the times he had taken me hunting and taught me how to use a bow and arrow popped into my mind and I silently thanked Lucy for choosing such an amazing couple to be my parents. We were together again after so long and I hung onto my father like my life depended on it. Newt was hovering behind us and I broke away to pull him closer.

'Everything's going to be okay now, Newt, we're a family again.'

Newt didn't need to know that he wasn't my real brother, at least not yet. I wanted him to bask in the joy of having his mother and father around again before having to deal with any more revelations.

'I need to check on my friends,' I said eventually, conscious that Newt needed some alone time with our parents. 'I'll check back with you later.'

We hugged as a family and a lightness that I hadn't experienced in a very long time flooded my chest.

Making my way through the buoyant crowds I marvelled at how Theo's father was able to save so many people. My parents had been reunited on the road along with hundreds of other families and they had joined the holy man's army heading back to Obanac to help defeat a corrupt lord. Thankfully they had arrived in time for us all to join hands and rid ourselves of the greatest evil of our time.

'It's great to see everyone looking so happy,' I said to my friends as I sat with them on a pile of rubble to watch the crowds.

I was still a little overwhelmed by my own family reunion and needed some time to process my thoughts. Plus, leaving Newt to some undivided attention for a while was the right thing to do. He'd been through so much recently and deserved to be wrapped in the loving embrace of his mum and dad.

'It won't last!' Fergus announced, folding his arms across his chest. 'It never does. Someone will come along to stir up trouble, and we'll be all *here we go again* and then we'll be dragged into saving everyone's lives again...'

Xander punched his friend playfully on the arm.

'Just enjoy the moment, Fergus.' I giggled.

'Oh, don't mind him,' Xander added. 'He's only happy when he's moaning, so this is a good thing.'

We all laughed as our friend feigned a shocked expression. It was good to be laughing again, and I wanted that feeling of peace to last for as long as possible.

'Do you think Theo's father is the best choice to look after the city?' Robbie asked as we all watched the holy man moving through the crowds, checking on his people.

'Yes, I do. He's everything a leader should be. He cares, he's honest, and he's got Theo to look after him.'

Theo hadn't stopped smiling since his father climbed through the hole in the city walls with an army of people behind him, and I loved seeing my friend in such high spirits. He had earned this happiness. We all had.

As I snuggled close to Robbie and watched the dawn of a new era unfold before my eyes I realised there was one person missing from the party.

'Where's Mrs Elrod?'

Robbie slid his hand into mine and pulled me to my feet. His eyes shone in the moonlight, and I was suddenly filled with dread.

'What is it?'

Everything was quiet out here on the track to the Link as the celebrations raged within the city walls. No lights polluted the night sky, and the stars shone unhindered.

I'd visited Mrs Elrod's hut thousands of times over the years, but today it felt different. Perhaps it was because I knew the truth about our family friend, or maybe I was the one that was different now.

My old friend lay in her cot covered in blankets, a cup of water on the crate beside her. Two of my Link neighbours tended to her as they wiped her brow and reassured her in soft voices that we were all saved.

I stood in the doorway watching the scene before me. She looked so much older if that was possible. I knew she was an old lady, but she'd always had this inner spark that kept her young. That spark had gone out, and now she looked so frail.

'Marianne, is that you?'

The ladies moved out of the way to give me room, and I sat beside her cot and scooped her hand into mine.

'I'm here, Mrs E.'

'Hello, lass, it's good to see you. I was so worried.'

'No need to worry any more. We defeated the phantom and everyone's safe.'

She squeezed my hand and pulled me closer.

'I'm sorry I lied to you,' she whispered. 'Lucy made me swear that I would keep you safe and never tell you who you were. She said it was the only way to protect you from the curse.'

'I know,' I said wiping the wisps of grey hair out of her eyes. 'You were my friend and my protector, and I'll always be grateful for that.'

The skin around her eyes crinkled as she smiled up at me.

'You are so much like your mother, Marianne. She was strong and beautiful just like you, and she was fiercely devoted to helping people. She would be so proud of you.'

I thought back to the fleeting moment when I saw Lucy Reign in the shaft of light, and I knew that Mrs Elrod spoke the truth.

'She would have been proud of us both.'

My friend smiled and let out a long sigh. I watched her eyes close as the final breath left her body and her hand went limp in mine. She was at peace, her duty fulfilled.

'Goodbye, my friend.' I kissed her forehead and wiped away the tears that spilt down my cheeks. I'd never known my real mother as I was taken away at birth, and my adoptive mother had been torn away from me years earlier. Mrs Elrod had stepped into the void left behind, and it was only now I recognised how much she had done for us; for me.

Robbie wrapped me into a tight hug when I emerged from the hut with a heavy heart and a red, blotchy face. Having him there made it easier for me to deal with losing my closest friend and as I sobbed into his chest, I knew I never wanted to be apart from him again.

'I love you,' I whispered.

He kissed me on the top of the head and circled his arm around my shoulder, guiding me away from the hut.

'I love you too, Marianne. I always have and I always will.'

We headed back to the city hand in hand, the sounds of laughter, singing, and joyful celebration filling the night air.

A new world was emerging, one that was equal and fair, peaceful and prosperous for all, and although there was a heavy rock of grief loading me down I couldn't deny the excitement that bubbled beneath the surface of my skin.

It was time for a new dawn without the threat of the phantom's curse hanging over us.

A time to start living my life the way I wanted to.

It was time to step into my power and shine.

BONUS SHORT STORY

THE

BLACK
RIDERS

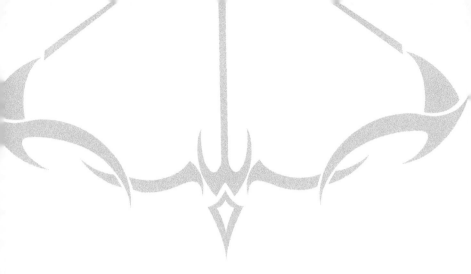

THE BLACK RIDERS

Leaving Marianne behind was the hardest thing Robbie had ever done. He watched helplessly as the Black Riders disappeared into the swirling portal taking her and Theo away to mage knew where.

In the panic that followed, Xander and Fergus half carried, half dragged him away from the city gates.

'We need to get Mrs E to Halia as soon as possible,' Robbie said, pulling himself out of the dread that threatened to consume him. Fear swirled in the pit of his stomach at the thought of what Crawford Reign would do to Marianne. 'Maz would never forgive us if anything happened to the old woman.'

'It's not looking good,' Xander whispered, glancing over at the cart which was being used to carry her away from danger. 'The threat of a hanging and being jostled around by the Black Riders has taken its toll on her.'

Robbie ran his hands through his hair and paced back and forth. He had to hold it together, but the terror overwhelmed him.

'I...I don't know what to do,' he said looking between his friends as if they could come up with a plausible answer. 'What if they kill Maz? What if I never see her again?'

'Crawford Reign needs her for his big plan, whatever the hell that is, so, for now, she's safe. It's up to us to make sure the rest of her people stay safe.'

Robbie nodded at Xander's words and patted his friend on the shoulder.

'You're right. We need to help her people—her brother. She has to have a home to return to when we rescue her.'

'That's right,' Fergus said, sliding his sword back into its scabbard. 'We get everyone back to the mountains and work out what to do from there.'

'Agreed,' said Xander and Robbie in unison.

They set off after the cart and the crowds of people who had, only a short time ago, been invited into the bosom of Obanac by a corrupt lord. The trap had been set, and they all knew the risks they were taking, but they had at least succeeded in their mission to free Mrs Elrod. It was just bad luck that things had gone so sour.

Robbie walked alongside the hordes of people journeying out to the plains and the mountains beyond and realised the masses contained a mix of people from all of the lower towns, as well as the plains. He even spotted a few servants from Obanac. Marianne had achieved the impossible and united the realm, and Robbie's heart ached that she wasn't here to witness it.

'She's strong,' said Xander, jogging up beside his friend. 'That girl can find her way out of any situation and still have time to save others along the way.'

Robbie chuckled and dug his hands deep into his pockets. 'I know, I just wish it was me with her instead of Theo.'

'Theo is a good lad, and he'll watch her back.'

'Oh, I know he will, he's proved himself more than once on that score, but if this all ends badly then we should be together.'

Xander stopped on the dirt track and grabbed his friend by the shoulders. 'Nothing is going to go wrong. The world isn't going to end today, tomorrow, or the next day, Robbie. I promise you that.'

They resumed their journey in silence, both lost in thought, the soft murmurings of the crowd washing over them as they trailed over the barren earth toward the lush vegetation of the mountain region.

Robbie saw Halia and Newt waiting at the tree line for them as they approached the foot of the mountain.

'Where's Maz?' Newt asked, searching the group for his sister.

Robbie looked pointedly at Halia, who nodded her understanding and moved off to give them space. He ruffled the young boy's hair and pulled him close.

'We got separated in the panic, and the portcullis came down before Maz could get clear of the city.'

Newt's eyes filled with tears and Robbie had to swallow hard to stop himself from breaking down.

'Is she dead?' Newt's voice was barely audible.

'No, just captured. Crawford has her prisoner, but we're not sure where she is so we can't get her. Theo was taken too so at least she's not alone.'

It was little comfort to the young boy, but it was all Robbie could offer him at this time. It was great to unite a realm, but it would have been one hundred per cent better to have reunited a family.

Newt rounded his shoulders and shook off his tears. 'She'll escape,' he said with determination in his voice. 'My sister won't let the evil lord win.'

Robbie smiled. 'I think you're right, kiddo. She can be pretty determined when she wants to be.'

Robbie left Newt with his thoughts and moved through the trees to find Halia tending to Mrs Elrod. The old woman looked pale and weak, something that shocked Robbie as he'd always known her to be the feisty spokesperson of the Link.

'Will she be okay?'

Halia shook her head and laid a damp cloth over the old woman's forehead. 'Her time approaches, so we need to make her as comfortable as possible.'

The old woman's hand shot out from beneath the shawl that covered her and grasped Robbie's arm. He yelled in surprise.

'Robbie, I need you to do something for me,' she said. 'I want you to take me to the Link and back to my hut. I need to be in my home when it's my time to go.'

'Don't talk that way,' he said, trying to lighten the sombre mood.

'I'll talk in any way I see fit,' she said, that spark of the old Mrs Elrod shining through despite her dire circumstances. 'I've completed my mission. It's all on Marianne's shoulders now.'

'What do you mean?' Robbie's brow furrowed as he tried to understand what the old woman was rambling on about.

'You'll find out soon enough, lad, but it's not my story to tell. Have faith in that young lass, and it'll all work out okay. I need to be at home though, and I'll need you to bring her to me to say goodbye. You'll know when.'

Robbie nodded his consent to abide by her wishes, trusting that all would be revealed in the passage of time.

'Okay, Mrs E, we'll get you home as soon as we can.'

'Thank you, lad,' she said, resting her head back against the wooden slats of the cart. 'You can drop me off on your way to Obanac.'

'Why would I go back to Obanac? The Black Riders took Maz and Theo, and they could be anywhere in the realm by now. I need to find them.'

The old woman tutted and gathered Robbie's hands in her own, her wrinkled skin smooth to the touch.

'Crawford will need Marianne within the city walls for what he's got planned, so she won't be far. It's your job to rally the army that'll fight with her.'

'Army! What army?'

'Look around you lad; you're surrounded by folk that will do anything to keep their homes and families safe. They'll stand behind Marianne if you ask them to.'

Robbie lifted his head to look at the people who had gathered in Halia's mountain sanctuary. Men, women, and children from across the land sat in groups talking about the sacrifices Marianne was making for them. She'd created an army without knowing it, and Mrs Elrod was right; with a little hope and direction, they would answer her call.

Before the sun rose too high in the sky on the second day, Robbie led Marianne's army out across the plains once again. They left Halia behind to look after the injured, who were still recovering from the latest attack by the Black Riders, but before they left, Halia had a gift for them.

'There's little point in being a mystical creature if I can't use my power for good,' she said with a sly smile. 'Hold out your swords.'

Robbie, Fergus, and Xander did as she asked and unsheathed their swords, holding them out for her to inspect.

She ran her hands over the blades, muttering under her breath as she moved from one friend to the next. Each sword glowed an unearthly blue for a few moments before she infused the metalwork with her light.

'What was that?' asked Fergus, lifting his sword up to the light.

'Just a little magic to protect you on your journey,' she replied. 'Should you come across Crawford's elite guards, your swords will be swift and direct. Nothing will stand in your way.'

The three friends gaped in awe at their mystical blades until Halia shooed them away.

'Go,' she said with a giggle. 'Save them both.'

They rushed after the crowds with a feeling of hope and inner strength that none of them had felt before. *Nothing will stand in your way*; Halia's words echoed through Robbie's mind, and he clung to them like a child to its mother's hand.

They marched in silence, covering as much ground as they could, passing over the dry and parched earth and seeing remnants of the villages destroyed by the Black Riders.

'If I ever see those evil demons again I'll cut them down and feed their limbs to the dragons,' Fergus said as they picked their way through the charred remains of Ely's village.

A deep rumbling filled the air, and the three friends halted on the track.

'I think you're about to get your wish,' said Robbie, watching the horizon as it began to sway and shimmer in front of them.

'Be ready!' Xander shouted at the army who stood at their back. As one, the men and women armed themselves for what was about to come.

The sky tore apart, and the Black Riders poured out of the grey portal, charging across the plains. Their swords glinted in the sunlight as they pushed their horses forward. Robbie counted twenty riders in total.

'Split up,' he shouted above the thundering sound of horses' hooves. 'Xander, you go right and take the right side of the army, Fergus, you go left and do the same. I'll defend the middle. We need to contain them, so move your teams until we can surround them.'

Xander and Fergus shot off in two directions yelling orders as they ran. The army broke apart and filtered into one long, impenetrable wall. The children and Mrs Elrod remained at the back of the party protected by guards.

'We don't let them break through!' Robbie screamed as the riders grew nearer. 'It ends here and now.'

Xander roared and lifted his sword into the air like a warrior general. The army followed his lead and bellowed their war cry to the heavens.

'The world isn't going to end today,' he cried.

The first black rider reached the wall, and the sound of metal on metal echoed along the line. Despite wielding his sword with all his soulless might, the rider was thwarted by wave after wave of soldiers.

The tail ends of the army, left and right, began to curl around the back of the Black Riders like a scorpion getting ready to strike. They circled the riders until they met up again behind them.

The Black Riders were now enclosed within an arena, and instead of fleeing for their lives, the men and women stood strong and defiant. No longer would they let these demons ruin their lives and destroy their lands.

With swords held high the army advanced, knocking the Black Riders from their horses and slashing at them with every ounce of strength in their bones. Blood flowed as the demons fought back but this time they were the ones on the losing side.

A rider flung himself off his horse and crashed into Robbie, slamming him to the ground with a grunt. He leapt to his feet and swung his sword in a wide arc, catching the Black Rider on the leg. The soulless beast screamed as the mystical blade cut deep.

Without hesitation, Robbie thrust his sword forward, sinking the blade into the Black Rider's chest. He dropped to the floor in a pool of blood and Robbie allowed himself a brief moment of celebration at seeing the rider's demise. He looked out across the plains and saw Xander and Fergus hacking down riders with their infused swords. Halia had saved them.

If only Marianne could see us now, he thought. A spark of an idea filtered into his head and with it came a feral smile.

The Black Riders dropped one after another as the army took full control. They still sustained heavy casualties, but when the last rider fell a great cheer erupted from the crowd.

'We did it!' cried Fergus, wiping the blood from his forehead. 'What now?'

Robbie addressed the bedraggled survivors. 'Marianne and Theo need us,' he said, his voice carrying over the blood-soaked plains. 'But we need to get inside Obanac to help them.'

Fergus and Xander looked at each other and back to their friend, realising he was hatching a plan.

'We take the uniforms of the Black Riders and we ride straight through the gates. Crawford Reign and his guards won't stop us because they'll never realise it's a trick until it's too late.'

Another cheer exploded from the army as they began tearing the bloodstained tunics from the demons.

They'd found a way inside the city, and now it was up to them to rescue Marianne and Theo from the Lord of Obanac.

'We're coming, Maz,' Robbie whispered to himself as he slid the black tunic over his head. 'I'm bringing you your army, and together we'll save this realm.'

ACKNOWLEDGEMENTS

Thanks to Sooz for being the most patient, understanding, and dedicated editor a girl could wish for. You continue to keep me sane on this crazy journey.

As always, thanks to my children and parents who offer me continuous support, love, and chocolate!

A huge thank you to the team at BHC Press for all the hard work you put into turning the inner workings of my mind into something special. Working with you guys is a true delight.

To the incredible army of book bloggers, social media addicts, and readers who turn the pages of my books—without you, I wouldn't be able to do what I do. Thank you for your support and engagement.

ABOUT THE AUTHOR

Shelley Wilson is a multi-genre author dividing her writing time between fantasy/horror for young adults and motivational non-fiction for adults, including her bestselling book How I Changed My Life in a Year. She was born in Leeds, West Yorkshire and still calls herself as a Yorkshire lass even though she moved to the Midlands when she was a child.

She is a single mum to three children and a crazy black cat called Luna, and loves history, mythology, castles, and pizza.

www.shelleywilsonauthor.co.uk